SHADOW

FURY VIPERS MC
BOOK 6

BROOKE SUMMERS

Stag

Mayhem

Digger

Ace

Pyro

Shadow

Wrath

Standalones:

Saving Reli

Taken By Nikolai

A Love So Wrong

Other pen names

Stella Bella

(A forbidden Steamy Pen name)

Taboo Temptations:

Wicked With the Professor

Snowed in with Daddy

Wooed by Daddy

Loving Daddy's Best Friend

Brother's Glory

Never worry about what could have been...
Always dream of what can be...

CONTENT

PLEASE READ CAREFULLY.

There are elements and themes within this book that some readers might find extremely upsetting.

Please click here for that list of potentially harmful topics. Please heed these as this book contains some heavy topics that some readers could find damaging.

Or go to www.brookesummersbooks.com/content-warnings

PROLOGUE

SERENITY

"You look fuckin' beautiful, Peach," I hear growled in my ear.

I shiver at that rumbly, gravelly voice, and my heart begins to race. I love that tone, and I freaking adore that he thinks I'm beautiful. I also love that he calls me Peach, I have no idea why, but it's something that makes me weak at the knees whenever he calls me it.

I'm in Dynamite, a club in New York City. It's owned by the Italian mafia, and it's one of the top hotspots to be at. As my sister is close to the wife of the man who owns this place, we've been treated like royalty since we arrived. We didn't have to queue, and we're in the VIP section. I prefer it up here as I'm free to dance with my girls and just have fun.

I lean back against the man and look up at him. Shadow.

The man makes me weak at the knees with just one steely look. I've known him for less than a month, yet he makes my body react in ways I never knew possible. We haven't kissed or even fucked, and yet he has this strange pull on me. It's as though we're magnets, drawn to each other. But there's so much more to him than meets the eye, he's smart, funny, and he always has time for me. He'll always make it a point to come and talk to me whenever he sees me, just like now, which I freaking love.

"Hey, Shadow," I say thickly. "How are you?"

His eyes are bright as he looks down at me. His tongue flicks against his lip ring. "I'm good, babe. You and your girls look as though you're celebrating."

I nod. "Yep," I say, popping the p. "My girl Esme is engaged."

His eyes narrow. "You don't look happy 'bout that, Peach."

I pull in a ragged breath, there goes my knees. "Peach?" I ask, needing to know why he calls me that. He started from the very first day that I met him.

"Your shampoo," he growls as his hands go around my waist. His grip isn't tight, but it's not soft either. "You always smell of peaches."

4

I smile. I love that he likes it. "Yeah, it's my shampoo."

"So, Peach, why aren't you happy that your girl's engaged?"

I sigh as I spin around and face him. "I love Esme. She's my best friend. But her taste in men is awful and her fiancé is an asshole. She's my girl, though, and she loves him, so I'm here celebrating with her, and I'm keeping my mouth shut."

"Why not tell her he's a dick?" he asks, his brows knitted.

"She's my best friend, Shadow. Us girls are stupid sometimes where men are concerned. I'm not going to lose her by telling her what I think. I can't take the chance that she'll end up hating me because of it, so I'll be here when it's over. I'll make sure that I'm here to pick up the pieces."

He nods, seeming satisfied. "I understand that, but is she really your friend if she doesn't listen to you?"

"It's not that simple. Esme and I have been best friends since we were in diapers. When you have someone that you love so much, you'll do anything to protect that relationship, and having the one person you trust the most come for it, it's going to hurt." I take a sip of my drink, hating that I'm going to even talk about the hardest time of my life. "I've lived through someone I love being so caught up in a guy that she didn't see them for what they were until it was too late. I couldn't help Octavia, but I'm going to be there for Esme."

His thumb and finger capture my chin and tilt my head towards him. Those steely brown eyes of his are fierce and filled with determination. "You're not to blame for what happened to your sister," he growls. "That bastard should have never laid his hands on her."

I nod, my throat constricting as I remember the pain I felt when my sister was in the damn hospital bed, after brain surgery. I thought she was dead. I thought that I'd never see her again. I blink furiously, trying to stop the tears from falling. This is supposed to be a good night, a happy and joyous occasion.

"So, what brings you here?" I ask with a raised brow once I've manage to get my emotions under control.

His smirk has the butterflies in my stomach swarming. "Now, Peach, that would be tellin', wouldn't it?"

I shake my head. I know what these men are like. They get bored of the club women and decide to come to the club to find someone else to fuck the night away with. "Horny, Shadow?"

"Wasn't 'til I saw you in that fuckin' dress," he growls, his breath hot against my skin.

I run my hand along his chest. "It'll look even better on the bedroom floor," I say a little huskily.

He flicks his lip piercing once again as he gives my body a once over. His hands tighten on my hips. "You want someone to fuck you, Peach?"

I press closer to him, my boobs squished against his chest. I hitch my voice a little lower. It's a lot more flirtatious, and a whole lot more husky. "Ending a night with an orgasm is always the way to go, wouldn't you say?"

His eyes darken, and he brings his lips to mine, not kissing me, just inches away. "You're playing with fire, Peach," he hisses, his cock thick against my stomach.

Good. At least he's affected just as I am.

"Sometimes, Shadow," I begin, keeping my gaze firmly on his, "I like the burn."

"Fuck," he snarls, his hand moving from my hip and tangling into my hair. He doesn't hold back. He slants his lips against mine and kisses me. He takes the breath from me as he slides his tongue into my mouth and dominates me. I'm only able to cling to him, holding on for dear life as Shadow shows me just how fucking talented he is at kissing. I can't help but wonder what else he's talented at.

He pulls back and stares down at me, those brown eyes of his dark and dangerous. "You're mine tonight, Serenity."

I grin at him. "Hmm," I purr. "Your place or mine?"

"Yours," he says. "I hope you're not working tomorrow, Peach. I'm going to enjoy my night with you."

My heart races. I've wanted Shadow since the moment I met him, and that hasn't changed. I don't think it ever will.

THE MOMENT we enter my house, he's on me. His lips slam against mine, and he kisses me hard. He sweeps his tongue into my mouth and makes me weak at the knees. I'm breathless.

I start to walk backward, my hands reaching for his zipper. I'm so damn horny. I need him. I need him to fuck me. I'm going crazy with the burning that's inside of me. I need to quench the fire.

He reaches for my dress and pulls it off my body. I'm panting as we break the kiss so he can pull it over my head. "Shadow," I pant. I'm so damn needy.

He gives me that cheeky grin, the one that promises me a good time. "Take your panties off, Peach," he says thickly, his eyes dark with lust.

I watch him as I slowly lower my panties and step out of them, leaving my heels on. His cocky grin turns into a full-blown smile as he strips down.

God, he's so fucking beautiful it takes my breath away. He's got tattoos all over his body. Full sleeves on both arms, his chest and stomach covered. I have a feeling that if he turned around, I'd see that his back would be covered too.

"On the bed," he snarls.

I do as he instructs, my body shivering in anticipation. He doesn't make me wait long. The second he climbs onto the bed, he positions himself over me, his eyes so bright and full of want. His hand goes to my pussy, and the moment he slides a finger inside of me, I release a long moan.

I run my hands along his body, loving the tautness of his muscles. I'm not shy about what I want and how I get it. Life is short, and you only live once. I always take everything with both hands and enjoy it, and I'm more than going to enjoy Shadow tonight.

I run my lips along his chest, tracing his tattoos with my tongue.

His finger is so thick as it pushes inside of me, and I gasp as my body accepts him. I cry out when he adds yet another finger, making my pussy stretch to accommodate him. He finger-fucks me hard and fast, and I pant as my orgasm builds.

"Please," I mewl at him, needing to come.

When his teeth graze against my nipple, I detonate, seeing stars. His mouth covers mine, swallowing my scream. I close my eyes and let the orgasm wash over me.

My eyes open when he slides into me. "God," I moan at his thickness.

"Not God, Peach. What's my name?"

"Shadow," I moan, wishing I had his real name.

"Exactly," he growls. His movements are slow and languid. It's too much. I need more. "That's what you moan, Peach—my fuckin' name."

"Harder," I beg him.

He grins at me. "Peach, you get what I give you." His voice is thick with need, his eyes dark with lust.

Fine. If he wants to be like this, two can play that game. Wrapping my legs around his waist, my fingers claw at the back of his neck. I need more. I need him to fuck me hard and brutally.

Lifting up, I press my mouth to his neck, my teeth nipping at his skin. I do it again and again. I hear a deep groan in the back of his throat, and I know that I have him. My fingernails press deeper as I deepen the bite. I'm going to leave marks.

It's almost as if I can see the control snapping in those amazing brown eyes of his. It's like a switch being flipped. He withdraws from me and then slams back inside. I bite my lip to stop the moans from escaping. Over and over again he fucks me harder and harder, until I can't hold back from crying out with every thrust.

"Yes," I hiss. This is what I want. This is what I need.

"Fuck, Peach, I'm not gonna last much longer."

"Yes," I hiss when he thrusts deep.

"Fuckin' come," he snarls.

My body tightens at his command, and within seconds I'm detonating, calling out his name as I do.

He thrusts once, twice, three times, before he buries himself to the hilt and comes long and hard, releasing a long groan.

He pulls out of me and gets rid of the condom. The man had me so worked up that I didn't even realize he'd put one on. I'm thankful he did.

I lie on the bed, my breathing ragged. I'm completely spent and feel thoroughly fucked. I'm going to need some time to regain my energy, but I'm definitely going to do that again.

"I need food," I laugh as I climb out of bed. "I think there's leftover pizza from earlier."

He watches me with a raised brow as I move through the bedroom. "Keep walkin' around naked, Peach, and I'll fuck you before we eat pizza."

My laugh is husky and throaty. "Is that a promise?"

His eyes darken, and I turn and walk out of my room. "Damn fuckin' straight it is."

SHADOW'S LIPS collide with mine, and I groan as his tongue sweeps into my mouth. His fingers clench around the globes of my ass as he pulls me flush against him. God, he knows how to get me worked up. But I'm drained. As much as I want him, I can't go again. I lost count of how many rounds we went last night. I'm deliciously sated.

THE MAN IS TALENTED. He knows exactly what to do, and I reaped the rewards last night and this morning. I've fallen head over heels for him. God, I knew there was something special about him, but I never expected to fall for him as deeply as I have.

HE PULLS BACK, both of us breathing deeply. Those amazing brown eyes of his are deep and filled with heat. I shiver under his gaze. "Gotta go, Peach," he says thickly.

I NOD, my lips feeling puffy from the kiss. "Okay," I say a little breathily. "Wanna repeat—"

"I'LL SEE YOU AROUND, YEAH?" he says, cutting me off.

· · ·

MY HEART SHATTERS. Fucking breaks at his words. I wanted more. God, I thought we were on the same page. But no, he's leaving.

"SEE YOU AROUND," I reply, my arms closing around my stomach. I'm trying to keep the hurt inside.

HE WATCHES ME FOR A BEAT, before turning on his heel and leaving. I'm rooted to the spot, unable to move. He's gone.

"STUPID," I mutter to myself as the first of the tears fall. "God, so damn stupid, Seri."

I WALK INTO THE BEDROOM. I need to change the sheets and shower.

I SHOULD HAVE KNOWN BETTER. I should have realized. Instead, I let my heart lead my head and now I'm in a position where I'm heartbroken and wondering what the future brings. I know what the men in the MC do, what they love. That's women. I can't imagine a life of seeing him hooking up with other women. The thought alone has my stomach rolling in horror.

No. I'm going to have to keep my distance—as best as I can, at least.

NOTE TO SELF: never get involved with a biker or anyone else who only wants just one night. I can't do it. I'll always want more.

ONE DAY, I'll find someone who will want more.

ONE DAY, I'll find the man who will love me back.

ONE
SERENITY
FIVE YEARS LATER

"Hey, Seri," Esme calls out as I enter my home and kick off my shoes.

I'm bone tired. I need sleep. School is kicking my ass.

I'm working at the museum, and I love my job. It's what I worked hard to do. There's an exhibit next month that showcases all the artifacts for the Rise of Industrial America Era, and I'm thrilled that I was chosen to head up the project. But it means working overtime, and it's hard to cram everything in, especially as I've gone back to school to get my Masters in Fine Arts, along with taking Art History. I learned that I have a love for all things that have a history. I find it fascinating to delve into an object's history and uncover where it comes from and who painted it or sculpted it and why.

"Hey, girl, you doing okay?" I ask as I enter the living room.

Esme's sitting on the couch with a weird smile on her face. "I'm good. Honest, Seri. I spoke with Harry and it's over. For good this time."

I watch her carefully. The finality in her voice comes as a relief, but this isn't the first time my best friend has told me that it's over between her and her douche of a fiancé. The man is an asshole who loves women. He does everything in his power to make Esme think that she's unreasonable, when in fact, he's out with God knows who doing fuck knows what. The man is a fucking asshole. If I had my way, he'd be as far away from Esme as possible.

She rises to her feet, her hands held up in a placating way. "I know," she says softly, "that you've never liked him, and I love you even more for trying to hide it and never telling me. But I'm done, Seri. I'm so done. I can't do this anymore. The constant cheating, the lies... I'm tired of it all."

I smile, glad that she feels this way. "You're always welcome to stay here."

She nods. "I know, but right now, I'm going home to my parents. I just want to be with them."

I get that. I'm close to my parents too. My dad especially. My sister and I are daddy's girls. Whenever we need anything, he's always the first to do it for us. My brothers are the same. They're protective and sometimes over the top with it. But I get it. With what happened to Octavia and that asshole of an ex of hers, they're scared of what could happen to us.

"You know my door is always open for you," I tell her as I pull her into my arms.

"I do know that. I love you, Seri. You're the greatest friend anyone could ask for."

"You weren't saying that last week when I was bitching at you to pick up your shit," I laugh. I'm a neat freak. I have to have everything tidy. I'm not sure why. My brothers are so untidy, it hurts to look at the mess they leave in their wake.

Her laughter makes me smile. "That's true. You're a pain in the ass, but I love you."

"When are you going to your parents?" They live over an hour away. I hate that she's having to go back to them, but I understand why she is.

She sighs. "Now." She takes a step back. "I'm all packed up and the car is filled. I just wanted to say goodbye. I couldn't leave without letting you know why and where I'm going. Please don't tell Harry where I'm going."

I roll my eyes. "That'll never happen." I'd tell the fucker where to go: straight to fucking Hell. Bastard.

She laughs again. "I'm going to miss you, Seri. Thank you for letting me crash here while I sorted my head."

"Anytime, girl. You know that."

Her eyes widen a fraction. "Shit, I almost forgot to tell you. Eric turned up today. He was looking for you."

Ah, speaking of a bastard. "What the hell did he want?"

She shrugs. "I'm not sure. He wouldn't tell me. All he would say was that he wanted to speak to you. I told him that he could eat dirt, but he seemed determined."

Great. Just what I need: Eric popping back up. I thought I had gotten rid of him once and for all when I broke up with him, but it seems as though I was mistaken. The guy is a fucking asshole. He tried to stifle me. He hated that I had friends and a job and always complained that I never had time for him, but whenever I'd try and make that time, he would go out with his friends. I got real tired of the constant insults, and I learned from my big sister to not let it slide. So I didn't. I kicked the fucker to the curb and haven't seen him since.

"I'll be telling him the exact same thing I told him the last time I saw him, Esme—that I don't care what he has to say."

She smiles, seemingly satisfied that I won't be entertaining Eric if he returns. Something I wish he won't do. I don't have the energy for him.

"If things get real bad with him, call your brothers, or even better, call Mayhem and Digger."

SHADOW

My gut tightens at the mention of May and Dig. The two men are amazing. I've known Mayhem since I was a kid—his woman, Effiemia, is Octavia's best friend. May and Effie have been dating since they were teens. Digger is Octavia's man. He's just as protective of me as my brothers are, but he's more dangerous. He's in the same motorcycle club as Shadow.

God, Shadow... It's been a while since I've seen him. After our night together five years ago, we went our separate ways. Thankfully, whenever I was at the clubhouse, he never had a woman, so it wasn't something I had to see. I'm not stupid; he's had other women since we were together, just as I've been with other guys. I just don't want to see it. I know that when he finally does decide to settle down, it's going to break my heart. It may have been five years since I was with him, but that doesn't mean I don't want him. I think I always will. He captured my heart from the moment I saw him.

I say my goodbye to Esme, hating that she's had to leave but praying that when she returns, it truly is over for her and Harry. I don't want to see her so broken every time he leaves the house. I know she wonders where he's going and who he's with. It's the worst feeling in the world not having trust in your partner. It drives you crazy and eats away at you until you're a shell of who you were. I hated

21

watching Esme sink that low, and I'm glad she's finally getting back to herself. I just can't watch her fall back again.

I settle onto the couch, my laptop on my knees, and begin to study. I have exams coming up in a few weeks. Everything is just piling up. I'm determined to do my best, and if it's too much, I'll repeat the exams. But so far, everything seems to be running smoothly. I just hope it stays this way.

An hour later, my stomach rumbles. I pad into the kitchen in search of food.

I hear the front door open and smile. "Trust you," I call out. "The moment I start to make food, you appear. It's as though you have a sensor."

My brothers always do it. Whether Octavia's baking or I'm cooking, they'll show up unannounced and demand to be fed. It's always the way. I happily feed them as it beats eating alone.

I turn from the stove when I hear footsteps approaching the kitchen. My words are caught in my mouth when I see it's not my brothers who have entered my home.

Three men, all dressed in tailored suits, enter my kitchen, fanning out, blocking the doorway so that I'm trapped. The tallest of the men seems to be in charge. He's standing tall, and the others are waiting for his command. They keep glancing at him.

He's pretty—if you like the polished look. He's

got dark brown hair that's slicked back. He looks like a guy from a nineties movie. The man to his right is stocky and has a scar that runs from his right earlobe down to his neck and disappears into the suit. He, too, has his hair slicked back. But it's the third guy who has me wishing I had a weapon. He's leering at me, his eyes filled with hatred and lust. My stomach rolls at the thought of him touching me.

"Ms. Michaels," the main guy says. His voice is gentle, but I don't buy it. His words may be soft, but his eyes tell a completely different story. They're filled with anger and hatred.

"Who are you?" I ask, glad that I've managed to keep the fear from my voice.

The smile that plays on his lips reminds me so much of what River used to do to Octavia when she'd ask him a question early when they began dating. I hated it then and I hate it even more on this guy.

"You're a lucky woman. Had you not been so affiliated with the Vipers, things would have been different. Now, where's Eric?"

My brows knit together, and I shake my head. What the hell is going on? "I don't know what you mean. I think you have the wrong house."

He advances on me. "That's where you're wrong, Serenity Lynn Michaels. I have the right address, and I have the correct woman. Now, where is he?"

I shake my head again. How the hell does he know my name? What the hell has Eric done? "I don't know."

I swallow hard as the fucker who's been leering at me grabs my hair, his fingers tangling into the strands. He pulls hard, and my eyes water at the pain that erupts in my scalp.

"I'm sorry," I cry out. "I don't know where he is."

I should have seen it coming. These men aren't here to play around. A savage blow to my mid-section pulls the breath from me. I double over as the bastard continues to rain blows over my body.

My face, my stomach, my chest, my head... Everywhere he can touch, he's hitting. The pain is horrendous.

"Stop," I whimper, feeling blood trickle down my face. My eye is closing, the vision blurry.

"Where the fuck is he?" he snarls, this time pushing me to the ground and kicking me.

"I don't know," I cry. "I don't know where he is."

He's not listening. He's angry, he wants Eric, and he's not going to stop. But I don't know where he is.

Blow after blow they rain on me, taking turns to hurt me. The pain is so bad that my body begins to surrender to the abyss.

Fingers tighten in my hair, and the fucker drags me to him. "If he doesn't get my money by next week, we'll be back for you. Fuck the Vipers."

He throws me to the ground, and I land with a thud, my head smashing off the tiled floor. My nose crunches against the tiles and blood fills my mouth. But the men don't stop. Kick after kick, punch after punch, the beatings are relentless. They're not going to stop.

It's too much. I'm in pain, and I can't keep my eyes open any longer.

I'm thankful when the darkness seeps in and claims me.

I just pray they don't kill me.

TWO
SHADOW

There's a weird vibe around the clubhouse, and it's been over us for the past week. Our vice president is moving to Ireland and starting a new chapter of the Fury Vipers there. I'm happy for Pyro. The man fell in love, and Chloe is perfect for him. My brothers are falling one by one, and I'm glad they have that happiness.

I wouldn't want anyone to deal with the shit in my life. I've kept my past separate from my brothers, and I've managed to make sure none of my family comes near the Vipers. This is the best for everyone. But as much as I keep everyone at arm's length, one woman got through. Serenity Michaels. It's been five years since I had her, and I've not once forgotten her. She's all I fucking think of. If I had it in me to make her happy, I'd claim her in a fucking heartbeat. She's sexy, beautiful, funny, and smart. She's the full package, and I she'll make any man happy. I just can't give her that. Not with my past. Not with who I am. I'll taint her. Make her twisted inside and feel the pain just like everyone else.

"You good?" I ask Wrath as we move toward the exit of the clubhouse.

"I'm good, brother. It's fucked up that he's pressing charges. He's fucking lucky he got broken bones," he snarls, his jaw clenching.

He's not wrong. A judge turned up at Hayley's place last month and tried to take her daughter from her. I don't know the full story, but Hayley called Ace, freaking the fuck out. With her brother in Ireland, she had to rely on the club to help her. She's family, and we step up whenever we're needed, especially for one of our own. When Wrath found out what the judge was doing, especially when he saw the bruises on Hayley's wrist from where the bastard touched her, he lost his mind and paid the fucker a visit, making sure he knew what would happen if he went near Hayley again. The asshole ended up in hospital and is now pressing charges against Wrath. He's also said that it'll prove that Hayley's an unfit mother by having criminals around her child.

Tonight, Wrath leaves the city. He's boarding a plane and heading to Ireland, where he'll become a patched member of the Dublin chapter. It's the best thing for him. If he's picked up for what he did to the attorney, he's facing hard time, and that's not something we'll allow to happen. Besides, Hayley is moving too. She wants to be close to Pyro. She wants her daughter, Eva, to be near her uncle, and she loves Pyro's woman too. It's the best decision for her and her girl.

We walk outside just in time for Raptor to make his announcement that he'll be moving to become Pyro's VP. It was voted on. Everyone needed to agree to him going, and with how tight he and Pyro are, it made sense for him to become the Dublin chapter's vice president. Pyro trusts him and he gets along with Chloe.

Octavia's cell ringing cuts through everyone's chatter.

"Hey, Seri," she answers with a smile. The Michaels sisters are close. "What?" she hisses, and my gut clenches. "Oh my god, are you okay? Where are you?" she asks, her voice trembling. "I'm on my way. Stay where you are. God, Seri, are you sure you're okay? Should I take you to the hospital?"

I move quickly, getting close to her. I need to know what the fuck happened. I'm going with her. I need to know that she's okay.

"I'm drivin'," I say through clenched teeth. "Where we goin'?"

Tavia blinks, her eyes filled with tears. "Oh, um, what about the kids?"

"Go," Eda says. Our president's old lady is watching her friend with so much worry. "We've got them. They're safe. Go. Tobias is calling Digger. Go to Serenity, Tavia. We've got your babies."

That's all Octavia needs to hear. She runs toward the car, and I'm impressed by her speed. Then again, her sister's hurt. I keep close to her, hating that she's fucking crying. Octavia's pure and sweet, one of the sweetest women you'll ever meet, and has so much love for everyone. Knowing how upset she is, it makes my stomach tighten. What the fuck has happened to Serenity?

I slide into the driver's side of the SUV as Octavia climbs into the passenger's side. "Talk to me," I demand, my grip on the steering wheel tight. There's a storm brewing inside of me.

"She's shaken up. She didn't say much other than she's hurt. She's in the kitchen, and she's hurt," Octavia whispers, her lip trembling as she speaks. "I don't know what happened. She's holding something back. Shadow, she won't tell me what happened. I'm so worried about her."

I push my foot down on the accelerator and drive, speeding past cars. I need to get to her. Never have I felt such a consuming fear as not knowing what's happening with Serenity. It seems every fucker is driving through the city today, not to mention every fucking traffic light turns red when I approach.

I'm out of the car the moment I turn the engine off, Octavia right behind me as I enter Serenity's house. "Peach?" I call out.

I hear a whimper, and my gut clenches and my jaw tightens.

"Seri," Octavia calls out. "It's just me and Shadow. Where are you?"

"Tavia?" I hear the fear in her voice. She's timid, and that's not Serenity. The woman would take on the world with a smile and flirt her way through it. She's happy and the life of the party.

"Yeah, Seri, it's me. Where are you?" Octavia asks as we move through the house.

My entire body tightens when I see Serenity walk out of the kitchen. She's clutching her side, barely able to stay upright, her face hidden behind her brown hair. Something is wrong. So fucking wrong. Octavia makes a move to run to her, but I hold her back. I don't want her to touch Serenity. Not right now. I need to assess how hurt she is first.

"Serenity, look at me," I say, my voice filled with barely concealed anger.

Serenity shakes her head, a whimper escaping her as she does.

"Peach," I whisper, my voice hoarse.

She raises her head, and my breath leaves me. It's as though someone has sucker punched me. Her face is battered, her eye is puffy and I'm not even sure that she can see out of it. Her nose is swollen and covered in blood. It's broken, that much I know for sure. Her lip is split open, and she's got bruising on her arms.

"Christ," I breathe. "Peach, what happened?"

She shakes her head as she falls against the door-frame. She's leaning heavily against it, as though she's unable to hold herself up.

"I can't," she whispers. "It's too much."

I step toward her, needing to hold her, to catch her. She's about ready to fall, and I'll be damned if she does it alone. Her knees buckle just as I reach for her. I pull her into my arms, and fuck... It feels so good to have her back in them again.

"Talk to me, Peach," I say, needing to keep her awake.

"Hurts," she whimpers.

I turn my gaze to Octavia. "We're goin' to the hospital," I growl. "You're drivin'."

She doesn't argue with me. She turns on her heel and races out of the house. I'm right behind her. Every step I take with Serenity in my arms jostles her, causing her to cry out in pain.

Fuck. I hate that I'm hurting her, but I need to

carry her. There's no way she'll make it to the car by herself.

When I find out who the fuck did this, I'm going to kill them.

I manage to get her into the vehicle without hurting her more than I already have. The second we're secure, Octavia drives us toward the hospital.

"I'm sorry," Serenity whispers. Her head is on my lap, and I'm keeping her close.

"What you sorry for, Peach?" I question, wondering why she's apologizing.

"You don't have to be here," she breathes, her eyes closed. They're red and puffy, her eyelids heavy from the impact of whatever the fuck hit her. "You don't need to be here. It's okay. Tavia's here. We'll be okay."

My brows knit together. What the actual fuck? Does she think I'd leave her? "Not happenin'," I hiss. "The fuck, Serenity? I thought we were good?"

She doesn't answer me, but I know she heard me.

Octavia sighs from the front seat. "Men," she mutters.

"What?" I hiss, and immediately regret it when Serenity whimpers as she tries to move away from me.

I place my hand on her head, running my fingers through her hair as I try to soothe her.

"You had sex with her and haven't really spoken to her since. From what I heard, you made it clear it was just one night. Why would she think that you'd be wanting to stay here with her?"

"She knew—" I begin but stop when I feel Serenity tense.

"Yes, she did, but that doesn't mean it didn't hurt. Shadow, she really liked you and you played on that to get what you wanted."

I grit my teeth. "Your sister is old enough to make her own decisions."

She nods, but it's Serenity who answers me. "I am, and I've made the decision that I don't want you here."

"Fuck," I snarl, not willing to be away from her. "That's not happenin' right now, Peach. If you don't want me around when you're better and at full strength, I'll leave you be. But right now, the way I'm feelin', I'm not leavin' you."

Neither woman says anything. I know they'll be pissed but so fucking be it. I'm not going to leave her when she's at her most vulnerable.

We arrive at the hospital, and the moment we enter the building, Serenity is whisked from my arms. Octavia turns and faces me.

"Do not upset her," she says, her voice harder than I've heard in a while. Octavia is a sweet woman who doesn't curse and rarely gets angry. Knowing

34

that I'm on her bad side should amuse me, but it doesn't.

"I get that you're lookin' out for her, Tavia, but she's mine."

She rears back in surprise. "Yours?"

I grit my teeth. "Yes, mine."

"Does she know that?" she asks, crossing her arms over her chest. "My sister loves deeply, Shadow, and she wanted you so much five years ago, but you only wanted one night. So she gave it to you. She's different now. She's ready to settle down and find her happy ever after."

Fuck. "I—"

She doesn't let me finish. "I don't know what or who made you feel as though you're unable to love, Shadow, but they're wrong. You're more than able. I see the way you look at her. She means something to you. But she deserves to be loved unconditionally. So if you can't be that man, the one who will give her everything, I'm asking you to please walk away."

She walks away, not letting me say anything. But she's right. I need to find a way to figure it all out.

Easier said than done.

THREE
SHADOW

Sitting in this fucking hospital waiting room is making me crazy. I want to find out who the fuck laid their hands on Serenity.

"What's goin' on, brother?" Storm asks as he takes a seat beside me. "You look as though you're about to lose it."

I'm not a man that loses control. It takes a fuck of a lot to get me angry to the point I want to hurt someone. Yet the moment I found out something had happened to Serenity, I felt as though I'd burn down the world.

"Someone worked her over," I say through gritted teeth, pressing the palms of my hands against my eyes, trying to block out the images I have of someone hurting her. Christ... What the fuck is wrong with me?

"Brother," he says low, "what's goin' on with you?"

I shake my head. "I have no fuckin' idea, Storm. Fuck. The moment I heard she was hurt, I just needed to get to her."

The stupid grin on his face just adds to my anger. "You're totally fuckin' gone for her, and you're so blinded by what that cunt did to you, you'll never be able to see it."

I grit my teeth. It's been a long time since she was brought up. Storm is the only person who knows everything about me. He's my brother. The man I trust above all else. He earned that more times than I can count. He's had my back when others didn't. He's the reason I became a brother with the Fury Vipers.

"Jessa Davis belongs to the devil," he snarls. "That fuckin' bitch should have been put down a long fuckin' time ago, Shadow. You want Serenity; we've all seen the way the two of you are. It's fuckin' good to see you happy, and whenever she's around, you are. It's time for you to put the past to bed. If you don't, you're going to lose the woman who means the most to you."

"How?" I ask. It's been fifteen years and I still can't put that shit behind me. It shaped me. I am who I am because of that bitch.

"You're not who she says you are, Shadow. You're

fuckin' not. You think for a second if you were, any of the brothers would let you around their women or kids?"

"Doesn't stop the thoughts, brother." No matter what I do, the memories and thoughts are always there. Watching as Cerys died... Fuck, it's never going to fade. I'm never going to forgive myself.

"It wasn't your fault," he snaps. "Christ, Graham," he growls. It's been years since he used my first name. "Your mom killed Cerys. She fuckin' murdered her in cold blood. Don't sit there and take that blame on. Jessa Davis was a cunt who tortured you and Cerys. She twisted that shit and fucked with your head. The bitch is hundreds of miles away, locked up where she belongs, and she's still fuckin' torturin' you. You got to let it go, brother. You are not to fuckin' blame."

"I should have protected her." I failed her. I fucking failed to protect Cerys. "Now look at Serenity. Fuck, Storm, you haven't seen her. She's bad. Her face is a mess."

He places his hand on my back and squeezes. "You were fuckin' thirteen-years-old, Graham. What the fuck were you supposed to do? Hmm? There was nothin' you could have done. As much as it pains me to fuckin' say it, Cerys knew what would happen if she returned. She did anyway, and she took you with her. I'm sorry, brother, but she failed you. Not the other way around."

I don't answer him. This isn't the first time I've heard this. Storm's brother, Jamie, told me this when Cerys died. He was beyond pissed that she went back to our parents' house. Growing up in the trailer park was hell. People looked down on you, thinking you were scum because you came from the trailer park. It was those fuckers that would anger me the most. The fucking bastards at school would try and bully the kids from the trailer park, but they chose the wrong people to mess with. Some of us grew up living with the worst parents on earth. Whether they were drunken assholes or drug addicts, they were the same: they'd take their anger out on their kids.

Once upon a time, the people in the trailer park would look out for one another. When things got bad at home, they'd let the kids into their homes and make sure they were safe. Many nights I'd stay in Storm's trailer just to get away from my dad's drug-addled anger or my mom's drunk-induced psychosis. Mrs. Nelson was a single mom to three boys and made sure that both Cerys and I were taken care of whenever our parents couldn't. But Jessa burned her bridges with not only Mrs. Nelson but every other person in that fucking trailer park. She fucked up, and when the time came to pay for her sins, no one would go to bat for her as they would for the others.

"You and I both know, Shadow, that you'll never let anythin' happen to Serenity. As much as you're goin' to deny it, you fuckin' love her." I look over at him and the fucker laughs. "You do. You fell in love with her the night she came to the clubhouse and played Never Have I Ever."

I flip him off. I'm not in the mood to be joking around.

"Bro, I know you. I know that you'd fuckin' die before you let anyone hurt her. So why the fuck are you hidin' behind the past instead of gettin' what you want? Jessa's locked up. She's never goin' to see the light of day. She can't taint what you and Serenity will have. You need to realize that, otherwise you're goin' to end up alone and bitter."

"He's right." I hear the soft voice of Octavia and look up at her, finding those bright eyes of hers brimming with tears. We've been waiting for almost an hour and still no word on Serenity. "I didn't hear everything that was said. Just that you need to realize that you're going to end up alone. Serenity is my sister, Shadow, and I love her more than you'll know. She's not just my sister, but my best friend and my protector." She gives me a wry smile. "She takes on the world without a second thought and doesn't look back. She's such a free spirit that she'll go through life without a worry. But with you, she's grounded, she's happy, she's stronger than ever. She really does like you, and I get it, we all have our pasts. They shape us, but we can't let them define us."

Before I can say anything, the doctor moves toward us. I get to my feet, my entire body tense as I wait for him to speak.

"Ms. Michaels?" he says, and Octavia nods. "Your sister is awake, but she's in a lot of pain. She won't tell us what happened," he says, his gaze moving to me. "It would be beneficial if you spoke with her and got her to make a statement to the police. Whoever it was that hurt her, they did some damage without causing life-threatening injuries."

Translation: whoever worked her over knew what the fuck they were doing.

"What injuries does she have?" Octavia asks, her voice trembling.

"Ms. Michaels has sustained a broken nose, a broken arm, bruised ribs, and she's had to have stitches on her head where it was split open. Thankfully, the cut on her lip wasn't as severe as we first thought and didn't need stitches. Your sister is going to be in a lot of pain for the next few weeks. She'll need to have her ribs wrapped."

Fuck.

"Can we see her?" Octavia asks, tears spilling from her eyes.

"Of course. She's groggy from the pain medication, but she's awake," the doctor says. "We'll be keeping her overnight for observations, but if all's well, she'll be free to go home tomorrow."

She's not going home. She's coming to stay at the clubhouse. That way, she's under our protection and she's safe.

I follow Octavia into the hospital room. The bruising on Serenity's face has started to come out, all dark purple and black, and her eyes are puffy, but thankfully, I can see them. The bruising isn't as bad as I first thought, but it's still bad.

Her nose is taped up, and she has a bandage on her head—no doubt from where she needed stitches. There's still dried blood on her face and clothing, and her arm is in a cast. She looks as though she got hit by a truck, but fuck, she's still so beautiful.

"Hey," Octavia says softly as she takes a seat beside the bed. "How are you feeling?"

"Like hell. How do I look?" she asks, her voice hoarse. "They said my nose was broken."

Tavia nods. "It is. You've also got a broken arm, and you're lucky your ribs didn't break," she whispers. "Oh, Seri, what happened?"

I take a step forward and Serenity tenses. "I told you, Shadow, I don't want you here."

I cross my arms over my chest. "I'm not leavin' you."

I feel Octavia's stare, but I don't take my gaze off Serenity.

"Well tough shit," she fires back, but winces in pain. "Why can't you listen to me? I don't want you here."

"I know you don't, Peach, but I'm not leavin'."

She flinches at me calling her Peach and it pisses me the fuck off. "Go," she hisses.

"Shadow," Octavia says, her voice hard. "She's asked you to leave, now I'm asking you. You can wait outside, but right now, you need to not be in this room. So please, can you leave?"

I grit my teeth. Fuck. I don't want to, but I know that me being here is making things worse. I give a terse nod. "I'm right outside," I tell her and see the relief shine in Serenity's eyes.

Fuck. How the hell can I make things right between us? This distance she's putting between us isn't going to work. I'm not letting her slip through my fingers again.

Serenity Michaels is mine. It's time for her to know that.

FOUR
SERENITY

"He's gone," Tavia whispers, her hand clenching mine. "It's just us now."

My throat closes with emotion. I want to cry. I feel like breaking down and sobbing, but I won't. There's no point. What's done is done and crying will only make it worse. I breathe deeply, trying my hardest to stop the tears from falling.

"Thank you."

I can't deal with Shadow being here. I hate that he's seen me at my most vulnerable. But I don't want him to know what happened. If he finds out, he'll lose his mind, and that's not something I want.

"You love him, Seri," she whispers. "Why did you kick him out?"

My sister knows everything that went down between us. I had been falling for Shadow since the

47

moment I met him. The night we spent together just intensified those feelings, and it was hard when the night ended and everything went back to how it was. He acted as though nothing happened between us, and that gutted me.

"You're going to want to know what happened," I say as I try to move. Pain hits me, and I release a whimper. God, it's so painful. The drugs the doctors gave me are helping to keep it at bay, but moving jolts my body and the pain intensifies.

"I am, and you know as well as I do that both Tate and Benji are going to want to know too."

I press my lips together and instantly regret it. I forgot it was split.

"I know," I whisper. "But, Tavia, I can't tell Shadow. I know he'll be angry, and I don't want him to get into any trouble. Besides, he's confusing the hell out of me and I'm not in the right mindset to deal with him."

Her laughter is beautiful to hear. I don't want her to be sad. I'm alive and that's the main thing. "That's my girl. You can give him hell once you're at full strength."

"Where's the kids?" I ask her, hoping they're not here. They don't need to see me like this.

My sister has three kids—well, four if you count Rush, which I do—all of whom I love dearly. I don't want to upset them, and that's exactly what they'll be if they see me like this. Rush and Cage are eighteen, Ruby is eleven, and Serafina is the baby. She's five.

"They're with Eda and the other ladies. They're fine. I'm more worried about you. They're going to be worried about you whether or not they see you. If I have my way, you'll be staying with us at the clubhouse."

My heart races. I'm not sure if that's a good idea, and yet the thought of going home is just too much for me to bear. "I'll stay with Laken, Miles, or Grant."

She gives me a look, one that tells me to get real. "Seri, do you think that Tate or Benji are going to let that happen?"

I sigh. They won't. Tate and Benji are amazing men—they're Tavia and Effie's men, and are patched members of the Fury Vipers MC—they get along with my brothers, but they're more equipped to take care of me as they aren't exactly afraid of the law. My brothers are amazing, but they're more lovers than fighters.

"Tell me what happened?" she asks, her hand tightening around mine.

"I got home from work, and Esme was just leaving. She's going back to her parents' house," I begin. "I studied for a bit, and then I went to make something to eat. The door opened, and I assumed it was one of the boys. You know what they're like."

She nods. "Always turning up whenever they want food. I know, they're scavengers."

I smile. "They really are."

"Carry on, Seri. You're doing great," she encourages me.

"I should have known," I say. I should have known better. "Eric," I spit. "God, he's such an asshole. Such a fucking bastard."

"What did he do?" she hisses, getting to her feet. The anger in her eyes is something that I love to see. For so many years, she was so withdrawn and defeated, all down to that bastard of an ex of hers. River broke something inside of her. He beat her until she was a shell of herself.

I shake my head. "The men," I breathe as I try to move once again. "Three of them came. Tavia, they wanted the money he owed." My body begins to tremble as I remember the men and what they did. "They told me to tell Eric that if he doesn't have the money by next week, they'll be back for me."

"Ssh," she whispers as she strokes my hair. "They're not going to hurt you again. You're safe now."

"I don't understand," I cry, unable to hold back the tears. "Why did they do this? Eric and I haven't been together in over a month."

"I know," she says. "It's going to be okay. I promise, Seri, you're going to be okay."

My body bucks as the sobs rip from my throat. Octavia gently climbs onto the bed and holds me.

"Why did they do this?" I cry. I just don't understand why they did this to me. What do I have to do with Eric?

"We'll find out, but I promise you, Seri, it's not going to happen again."

I know that Digger and Mayhem will do everything they can to protect me, but I also know that things happen when they can't. Just like Octavia. She was under their protection, and she was shot. Sometimes it's not enough.

My tears continue to fall as Octavia holds me tight. She's promises me that it'll all be okay, and that no matter what, she's here for me. She doesn't let go. She's right here as I unload everything through my tears and sobs.

"I'll call Mom and Dad soon," she promises me once I've finished my crying jag. "They'll be angry that I haven't called them before now, but I know what they're like and they'd overwhelm you, especially as our brothers would be in tow, and you need to rest and recuperate."

She's right. I love my family. We're all really close, and having them around is what I need, but it's going to be taxing. Having five people try to dictate what's going to happen is going to be painful. I'm grateful Octavia held off on calling them and has allowed me the time to get checked out by the doctors and come to terms with what happened. I'd have hated to break down in front of everyone.

"Let me know when you want me to call them," she whispers.

"You can do it now," I say, my eyes beginning to droop. "I'm tired." My voice is drowsy, and I know it's only going to be a matter of time before I fall asleep.

I feel her lips against my head. The bed dips, and then I hear her footsteps as she crosses the room toward the door. "I won't be long," she assures me.

"I'll be fine," I whisper, unable to speak louder. I'm so drained. The crying jag didn't help.

I close my eyes and feel my body start to sink into the bed. I also hear the door open and heavier footsteps enter the room. The smell of sandalwood and tobacco hits me, and I know instantly that it's Shadow. I should tell him to get out, but I don't. Having him here while I'm alone is somewhat calming. I know I'm safe.

"I'm goin' to be right here, Peach. I swear, no one's goin' to hurt you again." His tone is filled with determination.

His footsteps continue into the room and stop just as I feel his hot breath against my face. I keep my eyes closed, knowing that if I open them and see him staring at me, I'll lose it again and cry. "I know that I hurt you, Peach, but I fuckin' swear, I'm not losin' you again."

I don't answer. I have no idea how to respond to that. What does it even mean?

I start to drift off to sleep, and the last thing I feel is his lips against the bandage on my head.

God, he's making me crazy. Just when I think I could be over him, I fall for him all over again.

FIVE
SHADOW

Hearing her sob was the worst sound I've ever heard. I've seen the worst of the worst, dealt some people the harshest punishments one could give, but nothing has ever affected me the way Serenity has. Hearing those sobs almost brought me to my knees.

"We've waited," Mayhem says, his voice thick and filled with anger. "Tavia, tell us what happened with Serenity."

It's been hours since we discovered Serenity was beaten. She's fast asleep. I hated fucking leaving her, but I need to be here to find out what happened to her. As much as it pained me to leave her, she's with her parents.

Octavia runs her hand through her hair. Her eyes are red, puffy, and filled with tears. "Seri's ex," she spits. The anger in her voice is something we rarely hear. Octavia is probably the sweetest woman anyone could meet. She's a high school teacher, and never curses and rarely gets angry. "I still don't understand it all and neither does Serenity. But three guys turned up at her house yesterday demanding the money he owes."

I grit my teeth. I had no idea she was even dating anyone. "Who's the ex?" I snarl.

"Eric. I don't know his full name." She shakes her head. "He was such a dingleberry. Seri rarely spoke about him, but whenever she did, it wasn't great. They barely dated and she hasn't seen him in close to a month."

I glance at Digger. What the fuck is a dingleberry and where the hell did his woman learn that fucking word? I see his lips press together. He finds it cute, obviously used to her finding words to use instead of cursing.

"Okay, Tav, that's good, but where the hell can we find this Eric douche?" May growls. "He's not gettin' away with this shit. He's the reason Serenity's in the hospital, so we're goin' to need to pay him a visit."

"I don't know. But if there's anyone who does, it's Esme," she tells us as she sits up, hope flaring in her eyes.

"Okay, so where's Esme?" Digger asks her,

throwing his arm over the back of her chair. The man loves to keep her close—not that I can blame him. She's been through the fucking wringer. Digger held her in his arms as she was bleeding from a gunshot wound to her leg.

The hope that was in her eyes, fades. "Serenity said she's gone to her parents', but I don't know where they live, nor do I have her number."

Well fuck.

"You know where this ass works?" I ask her. If it's the only way to find out where the fuck he is, I've got no problem going to his place of employment.

I watch as she wracks her brain, trying to figure out if she knows, but her expression is blank. Fuck. Yet another dead end.

"We'll have to talk with Serenity," Dig mutters. "She may not like it, but the girl needs to tell us everythin' she knows."

Effie comes to sit beside Mayhem. No doubt she's been overhearing what we've been speaking about. She doesn't even hide the fact she has as she gets right down to the point. "Look, the three of you going to talk to her isn't going to go down well. I vote we send Shadow in. He'll get her talking."

Octavia sighs. "I don't think that's going to be the best idea."

Mayhem's gaze moves to me, his eyes hard. "What the fuck have you done to her?" he snarls.

"It wasn't his fault," Tavia says. I'm shocked she's coming to my rescue. "We all knew how Seri felt about Shadow, and the two of them hooking up was always bound to happen. They're like fire, ready to combust. It was inevitable. But what none of us expected was for them to walk away without a second glance. That hurt Seri. She's tried to put a brave face on."

Effie nods. "Yeah, it was shit. We tried not to make it a big deal because Seri didn't want Benji, Digger, or Kale to find out what happened because the three of them are overprotective."

I stare at my brothers. Who I fuck is none of their business, and both Serenity and I are adults. Had I known how deeply Serenity cared for me, I probably wouldn't have fucked her until I was ready to claim her. There's absolutely no doubt in my mind that Serenity is the woman who's mine. I was just too fucked up in the head to claim her before now. But seeing her hurt and hearing her cry, I know I'm not letting her go. I don't give a fuck what anyone else says.

"Not to mention," Octavia says, "Serenity didn't want to come between you two and Shadow. She respects you all a lot."

"I don't give a fuck," Dig snarls. "He shouldn't have touched her."

Mayhem nods. "Yes, she's too fuckin' pure for this life."

I laugh. I can't help but bust a gut. These fuckers are jokers.

"You think this is funny?" May grunts.

"I think you both are forgettin' that Serenity is a grown fuckin' woman who is capable of makin' her own decisions. What we do is our own damn business. I don't need anyone tellin' me my woman's pure. I fuckin' know that."

Digger gets to his feet. "Your woman?" he hisses as he plants his fists on the table. "The fuck do you mean by your woman?"

I get to my feet. I'm done with this conversation. I want to get to the hospital and make sure she's okay.

"Mine," I say. "I'm claimin' her. It's been fuckin' years and she's all I've ever wanted. No one, and I fuckin' mean no one, is goin' to stand in my way. You got a problem with that, Dig? That's your own damn fuckin' problem."

I push away from the table and stalk out of the clubhouse. I'll be fucking damned if they try and put a wedge between Serenity and me. I'm fighting an uphill battle as it is. But I'm a fighter, have been since the day I was born, and right now, I'm fighting for what I want and I'm not losing. I never do.

I climb onto my bike. The need to be near her is

coursing through my veins. Having both Storm and Octavia tell me that what happened to Cerys wasn't my fault didn't help, but them reminding me that I'd never let anything happen to Serenity was like a switch flipped in my mind. They're right, I won't. I learned from my mistakes, and I'm going to ensure my woman doesn't befall the same fate as my sister.

Now that switch has been flipped, I'm going to become an overbearing asshole until I know she's safe and the cunts who laid their hands on her are six feet under. I'm not leaving her side while she recovers. I know she's feeling vulnerable right now, and I'll be fucking damned if I let her be that way alone.

It takes me thirty minutes to get to the hospital. The moment I walk into her room, I see she's awake, but her mom's fast asleep on the chair beside her, and her father's talking quietly to her. They both look at me as I close the door behind me.

"Shadow," her father greets me with a slight nod. "Didn't think I'd see you here again. Everything okay?"

I nod. "Know that you're here, Mr. Michaels, but I'm also goin' to be stayin' the night."

His brows raise slightly. "Seri, you too?" he asks her, but there's no anger in his voice. "What the fuck is it with you and your sister? Hmm? Both of you like your bikers?"

60

Serenity releases a soft laugh. "What can I say, Dad? We like to take a walk on the wild side."

I fucking love that she's not afraid to be open and honest. I have a feeling that she takes a walk on the wild side a hell of a lot.

"Oh, Shadow, you're here. Is everything okay?" Mrs. Michaels asks as she wakes from her sleep.

"He's fine," Serenity says. "Why don't you and Dad go home and get some rest. It seems as though Shadow's here for the night. There's no point in everyone having a shit sleep."

Even beaten and in pain, the woman is a force to be reckoned with.

Her mom doesn't hesitate. She gets to her feet and presses a kiss against Serenity's head. Her father does the same, although he's watching me curiously.

"Look after my daughter, Shadow," he says so that only I can hear him as he walks past me.

"I will. With everything I am," I promise him. No one is getting to her, not again. Not fucking ever.

He gives me a tense nod before he leaves the room.

"You didn't need to come back," she tells me. "Dad was more than okay staying with me."

I move through the room until I'm standing over her. "I don't give a fuck if an army was at your door, I was still coming."

She gives me a soft smile. She looks less drowsy. "You always were crazy."

I grin. "Comin' from you, Peach, that's a fuckin' compliment."

Her laughter is like a punch to the gut. I fucking love that sound. "How are you feelin', baby?"

She stares at me, and there's a blankness in her eyes that I don't fucking like. "What's going on?" she asks. "What game are you playing?"

"I'm not playin' a game, Peach. I fucked up when I let you walk away all those years ago. I'm done lettin' my past dictate my future. I'm all in."

Her brows knit together. "All in?"

I nod. "Yeah, you and me. I'm claimin' you."

Her mouth falls open. "I'm sorry, did I say I wanted to be claimed? God, did you fall and hit your head?"

I grin. "No. I just know what I want."

She raises her brow. Even with her messed up face, she's still fucking gorgeous. "Let me get this straight. It's taken you five years to figure out that I'm the one you want?" She shakes her head. "How the fuck do you go through life if you can't make a decision?"

This woman... Christ, she's fucking something else.

"Funny, Peach, but we both know you want me

just as much as I want you. Now, rest, babe. Your body needs to recuperate."

Thankfully, she doesn't answer back. No doubt if she did it would be another smart-ass remark.

"You really didn't have to come back," she says a while later.

"Told you already, Serenity. You're mine. I'm goin' to be here no matter what."

She reaches out her hand, her eyes filled with pain at the movement. "Thank you," she whispers.

I grip her hand in mine and don't let go. "You never have to thank me, babe."

I shouldn't have fucked around. I always knew there was something about her, but I was so fucking screwed up I couldn't think straight. If I could, I'd cart her ass down to city hall and marry her in the morning.

That's definitely on the agenda for when she's better. I'm not letting her go. If she didn't want me, she would have kicked me the fuck out both times I entered her room, just as she did when I first walked in here after she was seen by the doctors. But she didn't, and that shows me that she wants this just as much as I do.

Now I just have to find out who the fuck hurt her. When I do, I'm going to enjoy hurting them. I'm not an enforcer for the Fury Vipers for my charm. No, I'm a monster once I get going, and I'm going to enjoy unleashing it when I get my hands on them.

Serenity Michaels is mine.

Fuck... Finally admitting that feels so fucking good.

SIX
SERENITY

"You'll come and stay with us," Mom tells me, and I inwardly cringe. God, I love my parents, I really do, but I moved out of their home for a reason. They're a little overbearing.

"She's stayin' with me," Shadow grunts.

I glance at my mom's narrowed eyes to the unbothered expression on Shadow's face, before I turn to Octavia, who's watching on with a smile. Yeah, this is going to be fun. My mom is a mother hen, and she hated—absolutely despised—it when Digger had Octavia stay with him when she was hurt. She bitched about it for days on end.

"Excuse me, Mr. Shadow, but that's not going to happen. Our daughter stays with us," Mom hisses as she crosses her arms over her chest and gives him a pointed look.

"Lady," he fires back, "what's goin' to happen if those assholes come back for her? Hmm? 'Cause you sure as shit aren't goin' to be able to hold them off."

"Shadow," Octavia sighs, "you don't have to be mean. Mom's just worried."

He nods. "I get that, Tavia, I do. But I'm not bein' mean. I'm bein' honest. Tell me what will happen if those three men come back? It won't be just your sister who will be in a hospital bed. Or worse, what if they've had enough of waitin' and are no longer dishin' out warnings? What then?"

"I can take care of my daughters, Mr. Shadow," Mom says, but the bluster has left her. She understands where he's coming from and probably agrees with him, but she's stubborn to a fault. That's something that both Octavia and I take from her.

"Never said you couldn't, Mrs. Michaels. I'm merely tellin' you what will happen if those men return and she's stayin' with you."

Mom turns to me. "Really, Seri? A biker?"

I shake my head. "Not my biker, Mom," I say softly.

"Oh, honey," she says as she pats my hand. "You really shouldn't poke the bear."

I turn to Shadow and see the blazing heat in his eyes. "Keep it up, Peach," he growls, and my body tingles at the sound. How does he manage to get my body to react to his words? The man's a damn magician. I know from experience just how talented he is.

Christ, I thought I was over this. I guess not.

"Okay, so I think we have that settled," Effiemia says, grinning at me. "Mama Michaels, you know that she's safe at the clubhouse. You also know the men would never let anything happen to her. Shadow especially."

My mom sighs. "I know that, dear. Trust me, I know that those men would lay down their lives for my daughters, you included. It's hard to know that your daughters no longer need you."

"Mom," I whisper. "That's not true. We'll always need you."

Octavia's eyes are wide as we notice the tears in our mom's. She's not usually an emotional woman. "Mom, are you okay?"

She nods. "Just having Seri here has brought up a lot of emotions and memories."

My heart sinks. She's right. Seeing me beaten and bloody would have stirred the memories of what happened to Octavia. We almost lost my sister due to that asshole of an ex of hers, and it was the most painful time of my life. She is and has always been my best friend and I'd do anything to protect her, but where River was concerned, there was no helping her. The fucking bastard twisted everything and made sure she felt alone. She believed we would all blame her for what happened because that's what he made her believe.

God, if that bastard was still alive, I'd kill him myself.

"Eda and Effie have packed a bag for you," Tavia tells me. "If there's anything that we've missed, just let us know and we'll get it for you."

The love I have is more than I could have ever hoped for. I don't just have my mom, dad, brothers, and Octavia. But I have Effie and the old ladies from the Vipers, as well as Digger, Mayhem, and Shadow —which is a huge shock, as I thought he didn't want anything from me. I'm blessed to have so many amazing people love me.

"Thanks. I just want to sleep," I tell her. I'm still groggy—caused by a mix of medication and injuries. The doctor told me that while I'm recovering from my injuries, I'll need to sleep a lot more than usual. "Is my laptop and books at the clubhouse?"

"Yes," Shadow says, a little annoyance in his voice. "Your sister thought it would be best to have them, and as much as I argued, she wouldn't take no for an answer."

I smile. My sister is the absolute shit. "Thanks," I tell her. "I have an exam soon, so I need to study, and while I'm recovering, it's the only thing I'll be able to do."

Shadow grunts but I ignore him. He's determined about claiming me. Years ago, I would have been all over that. The way I felt back then, I'd have taken everything he gave me. But time has passed between us, and I'm not the same girl I was back then. I'm dedicated to getting my Masters and pursuing the dreams I have worked so hard for. I like Shadow, and I think I always will. I knew going home with him that night wasn't going to end in a happy ever after for us, but I didn't think it would hurt me as much as it did.

It took me years to get to a stage where I was able to move on. I felt pathetic to have fallen so quickly for him. But I learned from my mistakes, and I'm not going to jump into anything with anyone. No matter who they are.

Two hours later and I'm walking into the clubhouse.

"Aunty Seri," Serafina cries when she sees me. The little five-year-old runs at me, her tiny body slamming against mine.

The force of her slamming into me rocks me backward. Thankfully, Shadow's hands take hold of my hips and keep me upright. "I've got you, Peach," he growls in my ear.

"Why is Shadow touching Aunty Seri?" Ruby asks, a look of disgust on her face. She's at that age where boys just aren't on her radar and she hates any displays of affection, including when Tavia and

Digger do it—which is a lot. I'm happy my sister found a man who loves her the way Digger loves her.

"Because," Tavia says, knowing that either Ruby or Serafina is going to lose their minds if they're not told why soon. "Your aunt is sore and hurting, and Sera baby, you almost knocked her on her butt."

"I've got her," Cage says as he stalks toward me. The boy is eighteen and so much like his father. Right down to his actions. "She can sleep in my room," he says.

I turn to Digger and smile. God, I love his son so much.

"Boy," Shadow growls. "She's mine. She's stayin' with me."

"Cage, honey," Tavia says, trying her best not to laugh. "Your uncle Shadow is feeling a little protective right now. It's best not to antagonize him."

I can't help but grin at the looks my nieces and nephews give him. I thought Digger and Mayhem were overprotective, but those men have nothing on the kids.

Shadow doesn't care. He keeps a hold of me and helps me through the clubhouse. Both Ruby and Serafina are right behind us.

"Aunty Seri, what happened?" Serafina asks once I'm seated on the bed, her voice small. I hate that she's sad.

Shadow's standing in the corner of the room, his

72

arms crossed over his chest and his lips turned into a scowl. I sigh. I'm not sure what he's pissed about, but I'm talking to my niece. I need to make sure she's okay. "I'm okay, sweetie, just a little bruised. I know I look funny, but the bruising will fade and I'll be right as rain."

She pauses for a moment, her face scrunched up as she thinks. "Like my knee when I fell over?"

I smile at her innocence. She's the cutest little girl and we're so very close. "Yes, sweetie, just like that. A few weeks and I'll be back to normal." Or as normal as I can be. There's going to be a scar on my head, not to mention, my nose will be a little crooked, and I'll be in a cast for my hand.

"You promise?" Ruby asks, and I know that she's old enough to remember what happened to her and Octavia. The little girl isn't biologically Octavia and Digger's—neither is Rush—but they are their kids. Rush and Ruby had an awful upbringing. Their lives were filled with fear and pain. Ruby was about to be sold at the age of six, but thankfully, the Fury Vipers put a stop to it, leading to Digger and Octavia adopting the beautiful little girl.

"I promise, love bug," I say with a smile, wanting her to know that I'm okay. I hate that she's worried.

"Pinky promise?" Serafina asks, sticking out her little finger toward me.

I don't even hesitate. I lean forward and link my

little finger around hers. "Pinky promise," I say.

She nods, thankfully, happy with my answer. "So, is Shadow your boyfriend?"

I practically choke on air. I can't stop the wince as the pain of choking has caused my body to pull and my ribs to hurt. God, I've done so well trying not to laugh and I somehow manage to choke on air. What the hell is wrong with me?

"Christ," Shadow bites out. "You've gotta be careful," he chastises me.

"Don't," I hiss when he goes to touch me. I'm too sore right now. I couldn't take it if he were to help. Not yet. I need the pain to subside.

"Peach," he says, his voice low but filled with pain. "You're hurtin'. I fuckin' hate watchin' you suffer. Tell me what you need?"

My heart swells at his words. I look up at him, and I see the worry swirling in those beautiful brown eyes of his. My heart skips a beat as he watches me. God, even after all these years, he still manages to take my breath away.

"Shadow," I whisper, unable to say much more right now.

He steps forward, his hand sliding around my throat, and I swallow hard at the fierce look on his face. "Fuckin' beautiful," he says, and I know that he means that. He truly does think I'm beautiful.

My eyes fill with tears. "Please," I whisper, but I

have no idea what I'm pleading for.

"I'm sorry I hurt you, baby. I'm so fuckin' sorry that I didn't know what I was losin' when I walked out your door. I fucked up, Serenity. I'm not goin' to do that again. I'm all fuckin' in."

I'm utterly speechless. Oh my god.

"And Sera," he says thickly. "You asked if I was your aunt's boyfriend," he begins. I completely forgot that my nieces were in the room. God, I suck.

"We already know," Ruby sings. "You look at her like Daddy looks at Mommy."

Serafina nods. "Yep, like Ace looks at Eda."

Ruby grins. "Like Mayhem looks at Effie."

"Like Stag looks at Kinsley," they say in unison.

I look up at Shadow, and I see it. The fierce look in his eyes is the same one that I see whenever I see the men look at their women. I'm not sure when this happened, and I have no idea how to deal with it. He's determined to make me his, but there's so much we don't know about each other, and I'm not sure if I'll be able to trust that he won't walk away again.

"Does that mean you'll be living here?" Ruby asks.

"For a while, yes," I reply, ignoring Shadow's grunt of disapproval. "Have you two eaten?" I ask, trying my hardest to change the subject.

Ruby grins. "We have. Mom made us pancakes."

My stomach chooses that moment to rumble

75

loudly. "Sorry," I murmur sheepishly.

"I'll get Momma to make you some," Serafina says, and before I can say no, she turns on her heels and rushes out of the room.

"Be careful on those stairs," I yell after her, my heart racing at the thought of her running down them and hurting herself. This time, I'm able to bite back the wince, not wanting Shadow to be pissy again.

"I'll make sure she's okay," Ruby assures me. "I'm glad you're here, Aunty Seri."

"Love you, Love bug," I tell her.

"Love you too," she says with a big grin.

Shadow waits until she's out of the room before he helps me stand up. "You doin' okay, Peach?"

I nod. "I'm okay. I've just realized that I need to spend more time with my nieces and nephews."

He shrugs. "They know you love them. You've been busy. Don't sweat it. You speak to them almost every day."

My brows knit together. "How do you know that?"

He grins as he helps me out of my clothes. Thankfully, I'm wearing underwear. "I know every-thin' about you, Peach. I may have been a fuckin' idiot, but I wasn't stupid. I always knew you were meant for me. I was just too fucked up in the head to claim you. I still kept tabs on you. Fuckin' proud

76

doesn't even come close to what I feel about what you've accomplished."

I stare at him, my heart racing. Is he for real?

"Shadow," I whine. "You've got to stop this," I hiss. He's muddling my mind.

He grins at me, and of course it's his sexy grin that has heat pooling between my thighs.

"Why do I have to stop?" he asks, getting as close to me as he can, his cock thick against my stomach.

I swallow hard. "You're going to make me fall for you and I'm not doing that again," I tell him honestly as I reach for his t-shirt at the end of the bed.

Thankfully, he helps me pull it on and then helps me into bed.

"You're goin' to fall, Serenity," he says once I'm sitting up with a mountain of cushions behind me. "'Cause I'm gonna need you to catch up."

I gawk at him, my mouth open as I stare at his retreating back. "You can't say shit like that and leave," I hiss. He's driving me crazy.

"I'm gonna see about gettin' you food, baby. You need to eat."

I stare at the closed door and wonder what the hell is going on. It's as though I've stepped into an alternate universe. I have a sinking feeling that he's right. I'm going to fall, and there's absolutely no stopping it. I just pray that I don't get hurt again.

SEVEN

SHADOW

"What's goin' on?" I ask as I step into the prez's office. He's not alone. Pyro, Digger, Mayhem, Stag, and Storm are all seated and waiting.

"Take a seat, Shadow," Ace instructs. "We've got a problem."

I groan. "What now?" Lately, it's been non-fuck-ing-stop. It's all drama and shit I could deal without.

"Bubbles is back," he snarls, and I see the anger in Pyro's eyes.

"She didn't learn the last time?" I ask, wondering if the bitch has a death wish. Less than two months ago, she got her ass handed to her by Pyro's woman, Chloe, and now the fucking bitch is back.

"Seems as though she hasn't. She's not stepped foot in the clubhouse, but she's on the grounds, and that's enough to make me want to slit her throat," Pyro growls.

"However." Ace grins. "She's visitin' with Pepper, who's currently being watched by Chloe and Eda."

I chuckle. "And Bubbles is still there?" I ask, wondering if the bitch has something wrong with her. Both Eda and Chloe would beat the crap out of her on any given day, so I'm surprised she's stayed this long.

"Yeah, but that's not the problem," Ace says. "From what Eda and Chloe have said, Pepper's in labor."

Fuck. That bitch has been a fucking drain on Preacher since we found out she was pregnant. She didn't want to tell anyone who the father was, wanted to string us along until the time was right. Turns out, the baby belongs to Preach. God fucking help the guy. I'd hate to be saddled with a baby mamma like her for the rest of my life. If it were me, I'd off the bitch the moment the baby's born.

"We're goin' to have to get the doctor here," Stag says.

"No," Py growls. "The bitch has caused enough trouble as it is."

"Py, I get that," I say, understanding the anger. "But this is Preach's kid. Yeah, the bitch has been fuckin' anyone she could get her hands on and takin' God knows what drug while pregnant, not to mention drinkin' herself into a stupor most nights. But we need a doctor; not for her, but for the baby."

He grits his teeth. "Fuck. You're right. Call the doc. I'd also have Effie there in case you need her."

She's a nurse, and she works with kids. I don't know how much help she's going to be with a newborn, but it's better than nothing.

"If we need to, we can take the baby to the hospital. As fucked up as it is, we can't trust that bitch not to harm the baby or claim we've done somethin' to her," Ace says as he runs a hand through his hair. "This is the last thing Eda and Effie need. The women are pregnant and they don't need to see what happens once Pepper gives birth."

The baby is going to be taken from her, and she won't be able to see it again.

"Where's Preach?" I ask, wondering how my brother is doing. This shit has got to be fucking with his head, but it must also come as a relief. The bitch threatened to kill the baby if he didn't do what she asked.

"He's with the women," May tells us. "He's makin' sure those bitches don't do anything to our women. Raptor's with him right now."

I nod. "You need me?" I ask. I'd rather be with Serenity, but I know my brothers may need me today.

"Yes," Ace says, and I hear the regret in his voice.

"I know your woman's hurt, Shadow, and if this shit wasn't happenin', I'd leave you with her. But the brothers are about to go on a run, and I need you to be with Preach, Raptor, and I."

I nod. "I'm there."

He gets to his feet and nods. "May, Stag, Dig, you'll take Cruz, Storm, Rush, and Cage with you. I need you to get this shit done and then be back by tonight."

"We'll be leavin' in thirty, Prez," he assures Ace. "We'll be a few hours. It shouldn't take long."

I watch as the men leave the office. "What's goin' on?" I ask, wondering why there's a run today.

"Got a call from Phantom," he tells me. "The new bar we have, turns out the manager is runnin' a fucking whorehouse from there."

Christ. We're trying to go straight. To get everything we can legalized, turning away from running guns like the prez before Ace. But fuck, some asshole who's being paid by us takes advantage, that's a fucking huge no. "Shame, I'm here babysitting that fucking bitch, Pepper. I'd have loved to unleash some anger."

Prez chuckles. "Trust me, Shadow, I know the feelin', but havin' you that far away from Serenity wasn't ever goin' to happen. As much as you'd love to hurt someone, you're not gonna wanna be hours away from her."

I fucking hate how well he knows me. But he's right. I'm not going too far from her.

He slaps me on the back. "Let's go see what the fuck's happenin' with Pepper."

"You're such a fuckin' bitch, Bubbles," I hear Preach shout as we near the outbuilding. It's where we've put Pepper up since we discovered the bitch had been taking drugs and drinking her way through the pregnancy. She was also having unprotected sex with men, most of whom were unidentifiable to us. She was doing everything she could to harm the baby, and that shit's just not fucking happening.

We enter the small outbuilding that's been made into a home. It has everything you would need to live. It's small but perfect for someone who needs a roof over their head. It was the only place we could have Pepper. No one trusted her to be anywhere else.

The doctor is already here, as is Effie. Pepper's in the throes of labor, and Bubbles is doing nothing to support the bitch. No, that's Chloe. Pyro's woman has Pepper against her chest and is helping her through the pain. She's coaching her through her breathing techniques.

"What the fuck is goin' on?" Ace snarls as we see Preacher and Bubbles square off.

"She needs to leave," Chloe hisses, her eyes flashing with anger, her Irish accent thick and heavy. "She's no help to anyone. If she's not removed, I'm going to remind the whore of what happened the last time she pissed me off."

I smile. "No one's goin' to stop you," I quip. No, every brother would love to see her beat the fuck out of Bubbles.

"Right now," she says, "Pepper needs me, and that bitch needs to leave."

"I'm not going anywhere," Bubbles screeches as she stamps her foot on the floor. "I'm here to support my friend."

"Yeah, by giving a pregnant woman in labor, vodka," Eda spits. "Not to mention, you've got cocaine in your purse. What the fuck did you think was going to happen? You'd celebrate once the baby was born?"

Bubbles laughs. The woman had been a club whore here for years, but she fucked up by trying to get pregnant. She thought that by trapping a brother she'd become an old lady. No one would ever make her one, and she wasn't happy about it. Thankfully, her plan failed, but Pepper's didn't. "No, it wasn't for after the baby's born. She's in pain. She needs something to help her."

Christ. This bitch. God, she's so fucking vile.

"It's time for you to leave," Preacher snarls. The man's had enough. He's dealt with this shit the entire time that Pepper's been in labor. Today is finally the day that this shit will stop, and he'll be able to breathe easier.

"No," she cries as he wraps his hand around her wrist and pulls her outside. I chuckle as he throws her outside and slams the door in her face, before flipping the lock.

She's done. She's not allowed back on these grounds again. She was only allowed due to her being Pepper's friend, and Eda and Effie persuaded the prez that Pepper needed her friend during labor. But they were wrong. Nobody needs that bitch in their life. She's fucking toxic.

"She's crowning," the doctor announces, and Effie and Eda move to help. I've no fucking idea what crowning means, but I'm guessing it means it's showtime.

Thirty minutes later and Preacher's holding his baby boy in his arms, while the women and the doctor tend to Pepper. I hadn't noticed before, but the woman is so fucking out of it that she's sky high. The bitch was drugged up while in labor.

"Preach," Effie says softly as she smiles at him.

I've never seen my brother besotted by anything in my life. The man has literally fallen in love with his son.

"Preach," Effie says again, and my brother looks at her. "I think it would be best if we take your son to the hospital, just to be checked over."

"What's goin' on, Effie?" Prez demands. "Give it to us straight."

"I can't be sure," she begins. "But the high pitch cries, the blotchy skin, it's not normal. It could be something more serious and I'd rather the baby get checked out and it be nothing, than we leave it and then it turns serious."

Effiemia is a nurse. If she's pushing for the baby to go to the hospital, then that's what we're going to do.

"Let's go," Preacher snaps, as he stalks toward the door, his baby pressed against his chest.

"Go," I tell Prez, knowing I'm not leaving, not when Serenity's in the clubhouse recovering.

"What's going to happen with Pepper?" Chloe asks.

She's not been around Pepper to see the damage the bitch has wrought. The other women have and have had enough of her bullshit. Chloe is sweet and kind. There's no way she'll leave Pepper alone.

"Chloe, Py will kill us if we leave you here alone."

She shakes her head. "I'll be fine. I have the doctor. Besides, Pepper's not in any state to do anything. She's barely conscious."

Well that's down to whatever the fucker took.

"I'm in the clubhouse," I tell her. "You need me, call. I'll send a prospect over," I tell her.

She gives me a soft smile. "Thank you."

I don't know why the fuck she's thanking me. I'm not the one who's staying here. I'll kill the bitch. She'll also have to deal with Pyro when he returns. I have no doubt the man is going to be pissed that she stayed behind.

"Let's go," Prez says to Effie. "Doc, fix her up and stay here. We'll be back."

We walk out of the outbuilding, and I see the worry in Effie's eyes as she watches Preacher.

"Effie, talk to us," Prez says. "What's goin' on?"

"I think the baby's dealing with the narcotics Pepper took. I did a little research after finding out what she's been doing, and those are some of the signs of a baby being born addicted."

I glance at Prez. We both know what that means. If the baby's addicted, it means that Pepper was continuously doing drugs throughout her pregnancy, but the question is: who the fuck gave her the drugs? She wasn't out of the house and was only ever around the women and brothers.

"We're goin' to find out, brother," he says quietly. "When we do, someone's goin' to pay."

I crank my neck. Yeah, they are, and I know exactly who's going to dish out that punishment.

"Let me know what happens," I say as I watch Effie help Preacher put the baby into the car seat. It belongs to one of Eda's twins, who are less than a year old.

"Will do," he says and runs toward the vehicle.

The moment the car's out of sight, I make my way to my room. Serenity is fast asleep. The bruising on her face is still bad, but it's not as puffy as it was. It's going to take a while before it fades completely.

"Hey," she says groggily as I close the door behind me.

"Didn't mean to wake you," I say as I edge closer to the bed.

She shakes her head. "You didn't. I was just resting my eyes."

God, she's a damn liar. Her voice is thick with sleep and her eyes are droopy. She was asleep until I woke her. "You good or do you need a pain pill?"

"I'm good, thanks. Are you okay?"

I gently climb onto the bed beside her. "I'm good, Peach. Sleep, baby."

It doesn't take her long to fall back to sleep.

Never have I felt so content in my life. I told her earlier that I fucked up by walking away and it's true. I should have got my head out of my ass a long time ago. Instead, I wasted five years. I could have had her sweetness in my life for five more years, but I was too chicken shit.

She's here now, though, and I'm not letting her go. Not fucking ever.

EIGHT
SERENITY

"What's going on?" I ask. Today, the mood around the clubhouse is weird. It's wired, as though anything could make everyone combust into anger. It's unlike anything I've ever experienced.

"Peach," Shadow sighs. "I don't think you should be out of bed." His hands are on my waist, his front to my back as he helps me walk toward where Octavia and Effie are seated.

"I get that you're worried about me, but being cooped up in bed is just making me feel worse." I lean back against him and look up at him. God, why the hell does he have to be so damn handsome? "You're so beautiful," I whisper, unable to stop myself.

"Babe," he says, his voice low. "You think I'm beautiful?"

I nod. He really is. Those brown eyes of his are stunning. It's almost as though he can see through my soul. It's the intensity with which he looks at me that takes my breath away.

"Serenity," he says as he turns me around to face him. "Do you know how fuckin' hard it is to keep my hands to myself?"

"What?" I ask, a little breathless. The man always manages to catch me off guard. I press my hands to his chest. It's hard to work around the cast on my arm but I manage it.

"You have no idea how fuckin' gorgeous you are. Watchin' my fuckin' brothers look at you pisses me off. They want you, but they're not goin' to have you. You're mine. The sooner they fuckin' know that the better."

"Claim me how?" I squeak, picturing him fucking me in front of his brothers, which is something I wouldn't do. I'm not into voyeurism.

He slides his hands up into my hair and gently pulls me closer to him. "Like this," he snarls, and slams his lips down against mine. It's hot, demanding, and heavy, but God, it feels so good. I moan deep in my throat, and I can't help but cling to him. Why does he make me feel this way?

I hear hooting and hollering, and he pulls back. My breath is choppy and those butterflies in my stomach are swarming.

"Shadow," I whisper, unable to say much else. He's got me hook, line, and sinker. There's no way I'm going to be able to stay away from him. He's like a magnet that is pulling me closer to him.

"For the love of God, you're mine, Serenity, and I'm not holdin' back any longer. The moment you're cleared from your injuries, I'm takin' every inch of you."

I swallow. "Every inch?" I squeak.

He gives me that sexy as sin grin. "Every fuckin' inch," he growls, his lips close to mine, brushing against them with every single word he says. "Anyone had your ass yet, Peach?"

My entire body clenches at his words. "No," I hiss. "And neither will you."

The fucker just grins. "Keep tellin' yourself that, baby, but I'm going to consume you. Every fucking piece of you."

He's doing a good job of pushing me to the edge. He wasn't lying when he said he'd be all in. He's not really left my side since he found out what happened. I don't want him to put his life on hold while I'm recovering.

"Just go slow, okay?" I ask.

He raises a brow. "You think after wastin' five years, I'm goin' to go slow?" He shakes his head. "Not in this lifetime, Peach."

I open my mouth to argue but he silences me

with yet another kiss. "Damn it," I say as he pulls back. "You're getting too used to that."

His eyes blaze. "Not even close. Now be good or I'll forget that you're injured and take you right here."

I close my mouth and glare at him. He drives me crazy. I spin back around and march over to my sister, who's watching Shadow and I with an amused look on her face. "Don't," I hiss. "I don't want to hear it, Tavia."

She raises her hands. "I'm not saying a word, Seri, but I will say you look good together."

Effie nods. "You really do. The girls weren't lying; he really does look at you the way our men look at us."

I huff and plop down on my seat, wincing as my jerky movement pulls on my ribs.

"Christ, Peach, be careful," Shadow says as he stands over me. "You're goin' to make it worse."

I glare at him, but deep down, I'm loving how much he cares.

"You good here?" he asks. "I've got somethin' to take care of, but I need to know you're good before I leave."

I've never felt so wanted by a man, so cherished. My heart melts at the worry in his eyes.

"I'm good," I promise him as I raise my good hand and touch his cheek. "Be safe," I whisper. I couldn't bear it if something happened to him. As much as I'm pushing against what's happening, it doesn't mean I don't care. I do. I care a little too much.

His brown eyes darken as he leans forward. He's silent, utterly silent as he watches me for a beat. "Don't worry 'bout me, babe. I'm good as long as you are."

Holy fuck.

"Go," I whisper, before I do something stupid and throw myself at him.

He presses his lips against mine. It's chaste and perfect. "I won't be long," he assures me.

The moment he leaves, the girls are all over me. "Okay, tell me what that was about. That man looks at you like you're his next meal. What happened to nothing is going to happen?" Effie asks.

"Oh, Seri, that man is head over heels for you. I've never seen Shadow so intense," Tavia whispers as she beams at me.

I shrug. "I don't know, he's making me crazy. I thought I was over him. It's been five years, and all of a sudden, I'm what he wants and he's not letting me go. It's beyond crazy."

Effie slides onto the seat next to me. "Listen, honey, I know that all this crap is a lot to deal with, but I find the best thing to do is focus on one thing at a time. Shadow's here, and the man's not going to let anything happen to you. So the question is: do you want him?"

"That's just it, I never stopped wanting him, Ef, but he hurt me when he walked away. I fell so deeply for him the night we spent together, and he walked away as though it meant nothing."

Octavia's eyes fill with tears. "I knew you liked him, but I had no idea just how much you fell for him, Seri. That was five years ago. People change, and in the time that I've been here, Shadow hasn't once looked at a woman the way he does you."

It's reassuring to hear that. I know he's been with others, just as I have. I'll never hold that against him though. I just don't know how to move on from the pain and hurt.

"Give him another chance, Seri. He's trying, and he really does care about you. If he hurts you again, then no more. Everyone deserves a second chance," Effie says, and she knows that more than anyone. She gave Mayhem more chances than he probably deserved, but I've never seen two people as in love as they are. Even after all these years, he looks at her like she's the reason he breathes.

"Okay," I say, knowing I don't have a choice. I'm already lowering those walls for him. I have been since he turned up at my house with Octavia. It's just hard to let myself fall deeply due to the pain of last time. But the girls are right, everyone deserves a second chance. Shadow walked away because he wasn't ready. He is now, so I'm going to try and take this chance with both hands.

I glance around the room and notice all the brothers are gone and only the prospects remain. "What's going on?" I ask them, knowing they're the only way I'll get an answer. "There's such an intensity in the air. What happened?"

Octavia and Effie share a look. "Okay," Ef begins. "How much do you know about the club whores?"

I shake my head. "Not much. I've met a few of them. Why?"

"There are two of them who are complete bitches," she begins. "Pepper and Bubbles. Both women are crazy as fuck and tried to get pregnant by the brothers. They wanted to become old ladies and didn't care who they trapped as long as they got the old lady status."

I scrunch my nose up. That's fucked up. Who the fuck does that shit?

"Pepper ended up getting pregnant," Octavia says. "The only reason I'm going to tell you this is because I don't want it coming out and you being blindsided."

I nod, my stomach in knots. Oh God, what's happened?

"Pepper didn't tell anyone she was pregnant until she hit month five of the pregnancy. She wouldn't tell anyone who the father was, but she said it was between Preacher and—"

"Shadow," I say, cutting her off. No wonder she wanted me to know and not be blindsided. I try to ignore the pain that's slicing through my heart. "Is it his?" I ask quietly, unsure of what'll happen if it is.

They both shake their heads. "No, the baby was born last night. It's Preacher's. But both Bubbles and Pepper are bitches, and they'll try to stir shit."

I take a deep breath, trying my hardest to hide the relief. It's a shitty thing to be feeling. I can't say I would have been happy if it was his, but we would have dealt with it. "Did they have a boy or a girl?"

Effie's face doesn't hold any happiness, and I'm curious as to why. Surely a brother having a baby would be a joyous occasion? "It was a boy, but Pepper took drugs and alcohol throughout her pregnancy and the baby was born with Neonatal Abstinence Syndrome."

My brows furrow. "What's that? Is it serious?"

"It can be. It's a waiting game to see if there's any lasting effects from it. The baby is addicted to the drugs Pepper was taking," Octavia spits. "It's going through withdrawal at the moment."

My eyes fill with tears. "Oh my god, what?"

Effie turns away, her eyes also wet from tears. "It's horrendous," she whispers. "He's crying so much, he's jittery, he's having trouble feeding, and the doctors and nurses are trying to get him to have milk but it's not enough. He's wanting a fix."

God... That's awful. I hate that the baby is feeling the pain of withdrawal. I'm not making a judgment on Pepper as I don't know her, nor do I know her story. But Christ, it's awful what's happening to the baby.

"Did they choose a name?" I ask.

"Preacher hasn't told us, but Ace and Shadow are going to see him this morning so maybe they'll get it out of him."

"Has he got everything ready for the baby when he comes home?" I ask, wanting to do something to help. I hate feeling useless, and sitting around while I'm recovering is boring. I need something to do.

Octavia's eyes widen. "That's a great idea. I'll have Tate call Ace and find out what he needs."

I grin. "I'll grab my laptop and we can start making purchases online." I love shopping, and I have a good excuse for doing so today.

Tavia jumps to her feet. "You stay there, I'll talk to Tate and get your laptop at the same time."

I roll my eyes. "Yes, Mom," I sigh.

"She's just worried about you, just as you were for her when she was in this position. Just give them all time. They'll stop treating you like you're about to break," Effie tells me. "Besides, you've got to save up your strength for when Shadow takes you again.

That man isn't going to let you up for air when you're recovered."

I laugh. "He didn't the last time." God, that was a great night.

Her eyes widen. "Oh? Do tell."

"Nope," I say. "Sorry, Ef, I love you, but I'm not discussing my sex life with you."

She pouts. "You're no fun."

"Shut it, you. You don't speak about yours either. If you want to know, then spill." Her cheeks heat and I laugh. "That's what I thought. Oh, is my cell here?"

She nods. "Yeah, it's with your laptop. Tavia will probably bring both down."

I rest my head against her shoulder. "Thanks for being here for me, Ef."

She kisses the top of my head. "Tavia's my best friend, Seri, which makes you my sister. I'm always going to be here for you. Whenever you need me, I'll be here."

God, how the hell did I get so lucky to have so many amazing people in my life? I lucked out, and I'm so grateful that I have them all.

NINE
SHADOW

"How is he?" I ask Ace as we walk into the hospital. No one has heard from Preach since they left the hospital last night. "Has he called?"

Ace shakes his head. "No, I haven't heard from him," he says, his words clipped. "He's had to deal with that bitch for so long and now his son is withdrawin' from drugs. If that was me, I'd be on a killin' spree."

He's not wrong there. I'm so fucking glad that it's not my kid. Not that I don't want a child. I do, but not with a crazed whore who is more focused on one-upping the father of her child. Being tied down to Pepper for eighteen years was never going to happen. I'd have killed the bitch before she gave birth. It's fucked up to admit that, but I would have.

I couldn't have a child with her. She'd ruin the baby before they could think for themselves. Seeing how she's already fucked up Preach's kid, I was right in my thinking. But Christ, whoever the fuck gave her the drugs is going to be in a world of hurt.

The nurse looks at us with disgust as she tells us where to go to find Preacher. Ace wraps his knuckles against the desk. "Thank you, Ma'am," he says with a bright smile. The fucker is killing them with kindness.

It takes us another ten minutes to get to the room Preach is in. The moment we enter the room, he looks up from the tiny crib his son is lying in. "Prez," he says.

I've never seen him look so wrecked. His eyes are red—no doubt he's not slept—his jaw set, and his blue eyes are swarming with anger.

"You good, brother?" Ace asks as we step further into the room.

He nods. "I'm good, just waitin' to see what damage is done. It's goin' to take a few days until he weans off whatever fuckin' drug she took."

I look down at the baby in the crib. He's a cute little thing. He's sleeping at the moment, and I'm praying he's on the mend.

"What's the doctor say?" I ask, knowing that the women are going to want to know.

Preach scrubs his hand down his face and sighs.

"That he's breathin' on his own. His lungs and his heart are good, but we just have to wait until the withdrawal passes and go from there. Fuck, brother, have you seen how fuckin' tiny he is? He shouldn't have to deal with this."

"He shouldn't," Ace agrees. "What that woman did was fuckin' unforgivable, and you'll get your justice, brother. Now, the women are wantin' to know what you need for when the baby comes home. They're buyin' shit and they're goin' to be doin' that whether you tell them what you need or not."

Preach chuckles. "Who's the ringleader?"

Ace nods his head in my direction. "Shadow's woman. She wants to make sure you have nothin' to worry about when you get home. She also wants to know what you're callin' the little guy."

Fuck. Serenity. The woman's banged up to hell and she's still thinking of others.

He starts to rattle off everything he needs, including a fucking crib. He doesn't have anything sorted. "We were supposed to have another month at least," he says. "Christ, I've got nothin' ready."

"The women will get it sorted," I assure him. "This isn't their first rodeo, Preach. Most of them have done it before."

He nods. "Tell your woman thanks, Shad, although, I'm not sure when you claimed her."

I raise a brow. "Keep your eyes to yourself," I snarl, knowing damn well the fucker's just trying to get a rise out of me.

"Now, we've gotta talk," Prez says without looking up from the crib. "I'm not accusin' you, brother, I just need to know."

"Okay," Preach says warily as he watches him.

"Pepper's been usin' her entire pregnancy. We need to know where she got the drugs. Did you give them to her? No one would blame you. She's a fuckin' pain in the ass."

Anger flashes through his eyes. "No, I fuckin' didn't, and what the fuck do you mean she's been usin' the entire pregnancy?"

I sigh. I should have realized that he didn't put two and two together. "The only reason the kid is like this is because she's been usin' throughout the pregnancy. He wouldn't be goin' through withdrawal had she stopped months ago like you assumed."

His jaw clenches. "I'm goin' to fuckin' kill her," he snarls. "What the fuck was she thinkin'? She could have killed him."

Prez nods. "We need to speak to her, but I'm guessin' you want to be involved in that conversation?"

He nods. "Too fuckin' right I do." He glances at

me. "Would your woman come and stay with Tyson?"

I smirk. "Tyson?"

He nods. "He's a fighter. Wouldn't you say that's a fittin' name?"

"It suits him. It's fuckin' perfect for him. And yes, Serenity would be happy to sit with him while you're busy—as long as there's someone with her."

"We'll send a prospect with her. She won't be alone," Prez assures me.

"I'll set it up," I tell Preach. "Once she's here, we'll head back and sort this shit out."

I walk out of the room and call Digger, who's at the clubhouse with the women.

"You good?" I ask Serenity the moment I see her.

She gives me a smile, and I notice the fight she had in her eyes the last time I saw her is gone. "Yeah, how's Preacher and the baby?"

"Tyson, babe," I tell her. "And he's doin' okay."

I watch as her eyes widen a fraction before that smile she has brightens. Christ... So fucking beautiful. "Fitting," she murmurs. "How's Preacher holding up?"

"The man's wrecked, Peach. His son's goin'

through withdrawal. How would you feel if that was our child?"

"I'd be so devastated," she whispers, not even blinking at my words. "God, it's awful."

I pull her into my arms. "It's goin' to be okay. Once Tyson's through this, he'll be home."

"Everything that Preach needs has been ordered and should be at the clubhouse tomorrow. Would you be able to help set the room up for him?"

"Of course. The brothers will help. We'll have it ready for when they come home."

She smiles up at me. "I'm sorry," she says softly.

I cradle her face in my hands. Just having her this sweet is fucking amazing. While I love the anger flashing, nothing beats this. "For what?"

"Pushing you away," she tells me. "I just don't want to get hurt again. But that wasn't your fault. It was my own."

"I swear to you, babe, I'm not goin' to hurt you again. You're mine, no matter what. I'm not lettin' you go."

She sinks into my embrace, and I hold her close. "That's good, because I think Effie would kick your ass if you did."

I chuckle. The woman would fucking try. "Okay, babe, let's go and introduce you to Tyson."

"I'm excited to meet him, but I'm confused as to

why Preacher wanted me to be here," she says softly as we walk toward Tyson's room.

"Honestly, I think it's 'cause you're not around often and he couldn't choose between the other women." The man's a serious womanizer. He hates upsetting them.

She laughs. "That makes sense. Okay, let's go and see this cutie."

I take her hand, the one that's not in a cast, and lead her into Tyson's room.

"Congratulations, Preach," Serenity says as we walk into the room. She makes a beeline for him and gives the man a hug. I bite back the snarl as he wraps her into his arms.

"Thanks, Seri. You know, you're the first one to say that," he says as he looks down at Tyson in the crib. "I hear you've been busy today?"

She shrugs as she steps up to the crib. Tyson's fighting in there, and I can see by the weird look that crosses all three of their faces that it's not right. I've only been around my brothers kids, so I have no idea what the fuck they're supposed to do.

"You need things ready for when the little man comes home. I know from when Ef had Elouise and Tavia had Serafina that it's hectic the first few weeks as you try to adjust. The last thing you need is to worry about stuff you need to buy."

"'Preciate it, Seri. You sure you want to be stuck

with Shadow? I could take you," Preach says with a grin. It's the first real one I've seen today.

"Try it," I snarl, "and Tyson's gonna end up an orphan," I tell him. We all know there's no fucking way that Pepper is going to survive the week.

He raises his hands in surrender. "Chill, bro, I'm just messin'."

"Let's get this shit sorted. Seri, the prospects are here. If you need anythin', one of them will get it for you and the other is to stand guard. Okay?" Prez says.

She nods. "Thank you. Now go, and make sure you get Preacher to shower and have something to eat," she says as she walks over to me. "Be safe," she whispers once she's close. I'm shocked when she raises up onto her tiptoes and presses a kiss against my lips. "Go," she says as she pulls back. "Then come and get me when you're finished. Maybe we can watch a movie tonight?"

I curl my arm around her waist and pull her even closer. "Definitely," I say. I fucking want that. I want her any way I can get her, but to have alone time with her without worrying about anything, it's the perfect night. "We won't be long, baby. If you need anythin', the prospects are outside."

"I will," she promises me. "Preach, is there anything I need to know?"

"If he wakes and starts to cry, ask one of the

prospects to put him in your arms. He likes to be held. He may also need to be fed, but the nurses will help with that. If you're unsure, call the nurses."

"Okay, thank you." She gives me one last look, and it's filled with worry, but I also see something else, and I'm fucking pleased that it's there. It's not love, but it's as fucking close as you can get to it.

I give her one last kiss and then we get the hell out of there. It's time to pay Pepper a visit.

TEN
SHADOW

When we get to the clubhouse, Preacher doesn't go in. No, he goes straight to the outbuilding where Pepper is staying. The doctor stayed with her last night, making sure she was okay after giving birth. She's fine. The doctor said she went to shower around four this morning, and when she came out of the shower, she was high once again.

I notice that Mayhem and Storm are heading toward the house too. "You good?" Prez asks them.

May shakes his head. "Nope. Got word from the doc. She's locked herself in the house and he can't get in. He didn't want to kick the door down."

Preacher doesn't wait for the go ahead. He lifts his foot and kicks the door. The fucking thing splinters on his first try. We follow him into the house, and I'm concerned by the lack of sound. You'd think a woman hell bent on not having anyone around her would lose their shit if the door was kicked in.

"The fuck?" Preach growls as he enters the bedroom. "Christ. Stupid fuckin' bitch," he snarls.

I move around Ace and see Preacher pulling a naked Bubbles off the bed. The fucking whore was going down on Pepper. The fuck were they playing at? The woman gave birth only twenty-four hours ago.

I stare down at the bed. It's completely fucking ruined. There's blood everywhere, all over the two of them. My stomach churns when Preach turns Bubbles around. The bitch's face is smeared with Pepper's blood. Christ.

"Fuck me," Preacher mutters. "She's dead," he snarls.

My brows practically hit my hairline. "Come again?"

"The bitch is dead, Shad. She's not breathin'."

"Can't lie," I say as I lean against the wall. "If I was goin' down on that, I'd fuckin' die too."

Prez chuckles. "Not much can shock me, but fuck, these women do every fuckin' time."

"Is that bitch out cold?" May asks, nodding in Pepper's direction.

"No, she's completely fuckin' out of it. The bitch is high as a kite."

Fucking hell. Never have I seen anything like this shit. I didn't expect to walk in and find a dead woman with her head stuck between another woman's thighs. Usually, that would turn anyone on, but not when there's so much blood and a high fucking bitch, along with a dead one. That's just beyond fucked up.

"Get her sobered up. She's got lots to answer for," Prez says. "I need her in some sort of condition to answer the fuckin' questions.

"May, Storm, burn this fuckin' shit. Shadow, call the doctor. He's goin' to need to sign off on Bubbles' death."

"Well, Py will be happy the cunt can't get near Chloe again." Mayhem smirks. "Now all we need is for Pepper to die and then everyone will be happy." He turns to Preach. "Congrats on the baby, man. How is he?"

"He's okay, just waitin' on the doctor to update us, but it's goin' to take some time."

May nods. "That's good. He made it through the pregnancy and the birth; he's goin' to be fine. He's a fighter."

Preach grins. "That he is. Tyson's a hell of a fighter."

"Fuckin' love the name," Storm hoots. "It's perfect for him."

"Let's get this shit done," Ace says. "The sooner

we have Pepper out of our lives, the better off Tyson will be."

IT TAKES Preach an hour to get Pepper in a decent condition. She's showered, and her eyes are filled with anger rather than the vacant look they had.

The house has been cleaned. I'm not sure who did it, but it looks as though it's never been used. There's no longer a bed, but that's for the best. We couldn't keep that shit after what happened.

"Do you know why you're here, Pepper?" Prez asks. We're in the other outbuilding, but this one isn't equipped for living. It's where we deal with those who have wronged us.

She shrugs. Either she's completely oblivious to what's about to happen or she doesn't give a fuck. Either way, she's fucking stupid. "Don't know, nor do I care. Can we get this over with?"

The blatant disrespect is just another nail in her coffin.

"Who's been supplyin' you with drugs, Pepper? And don't fuckin' lie to me. Your son's in the hospital now, goin' through withdrawal."

Her features are etched with pain. Finally, something she seems to give a fuck about. "Is he okay?"

116

"Like you give a fuck," Preacher snarls. "You did this to him."

"Fuck you," she fires back. "Look at you, playing daddy dearest. You're a joke, Preach. You'd do anything to make up for the sins you've committed, wouldn't you?"

He steps forward and she cowers back. She's not so brave now. "Told you, Pepper, that the moment you gave birth, your days were numbered. Guess your luck has just run out. So, why don't you answer the fuckin' question. Who's been giving you the fuckin' drugs?"

She glances around at Ace, Preach, Mayhem, Storm, and I. She knows she's fucked no matter what she does. She'll be better off if she's honest about this.

"The doctor," she hisses. "He was the only one who was nice to me. You animals kept me in a fucking cage. I couldn't breathe. The only escape was to take the drugs. You gave me no choice."

"Bullshit," Ace snarls. "You had every fuckin' choice. Had you chosen to be a decent parent, you would have survived to see your boy grow up. Instead, you're never going to even see him."

"No," she cries. "Please, Ace, I'll do anything. I want to see my baby."

Preacher shakes his head. "Should have thought about that, Pepper. You fucked up more times than I can count. Between the drugs, drink, the fuckin' men, not to mention the threats about cuttin' the baby from your belly, it's too late. You're done."

So is the fucking doctor. Once Ace gets his hands on him, he's finished. That fucker has been with us for a long time. I have no fucking idea why he'd betray us, especially by giving Pepper drugs, especially knowing she was pregnant.

"What was you takin'?" Preacher growls.

"OxyContin," she says quietly, but we all fucking hear her.

"You fucking bitch," Preacher snarls. "You're a fucking cunt, Pepper. You'll burn in Hell for what you've done to our kid."

The sly smirk on her face infuriates me. There's no doubt that if it were me in Preacher's shoes, I'd strangle the bitch until her neck snapped between my hands.

"May, go get that fuckin' doctor," Prez snaps. "Preach, end this shit."

Preacher reaches for his knife, swirling it between his fingers and whistling as he moves toward her. "Had you not given birth to my son, Pepper, I'd have no mercy on you. You should count your lucky stars that you gave me my son."

He doesn't hesitate. As he slices his knife across her throat, the only sound that can be heard is her gasping for air. Blood pours from the open wound, her eyes wide as her body bucks, trying to get much needed oxygen into her lungs. It's no use. It's never going to happen. Preacher cut through her trachea. She was dead the moment he did.

We all stand and watch as the life leaves her eyes. She fucked around too much to survive. She caused too many problems. The only reason she lived for as long as she did was due to the pregnancy. She should have known that the moment the baby was born, she was done.

Mayhem walks back into the building, the doctor at his side. The moment the fucker spots Pepper's dead bloody body, he blanches, his face white and his eyes wide.

"When," Ace says, his voice vibrating with anger. "Did you think it was wise to go against the club, Declan?"

The doctor's eyes widen even further. "What?" he asks, completely ashen.

"You think we don't know it was you who was supplyin' the whores with Oxy and God knows what other fuckin' drugs? What else have you been doin'? Hmm? What else have you done to try and bring us down?"

The doctor shakes his head. "Nothing, Ace. I swear to you, I haven't done anything."

Ace steps forward. "So you never gave the whores the drugs?"

Declan scurries backward, but unlucky for him, he crashes straight into Mayhem, who holds him still. "Answer him," he growls. "Did you give the women the drugs?"

"Yes," he sighs. "I didn't know what else to do. They needed them. I was trying to help."

Preacher's laugh is forced. "Help them? My son is in the fuckin' hospital fighting the addiction." He turns to Ace, waiting for the go ahead to do what he so desperately needs to.

"What else have you done?" Ace asks him. "Tell me now, Declan, and we'll have mercy on you."

He's lying. There's no mercy for what he's done. None whatsoever.

"Nothing, I promise you. I just wanted to help the women. That's all."

Ace nods to Preacher, and once again, he plays with the knife between his fingers.

He swipes his knife across Declan's shirt, cutting through the material and skin. It's deep, but not enough to kill him. Blood seeps onto his skin, and the fucker releases a pain-filled groan. He should have thought before giving a pregnant woman fucking drugs.

Preacher's knife moves fast, slicing at his torso, criss-crossing its way along the skin, as he leaves his mark. He's letting everyone know that Declan is a snake and betrayed us. Preacher isn't usually one to do this. That's usually left to Wrath, Mayhem, and I. But with Wrath gone, Preach is taking his opportunity. Besides, it's his baby that's in the hospital, and if the tables were turned, I wouldn't want anyone else taking my shot.

"Preach," Ace says an hour or so later. There's not a piece of skin left untouched. Preacher has sliced every inch of the cunt. "Get this shit done. You need to shower and get back to your boy."

He's right. He needs to end this. It's been hours since we left the hospital and Preacher's been going at him for a long time. He's been methodical, making sure he doesn't hit too deep. He's kept Declan alive so that he can torture him. But it's time to end this.

Preacher grins, flicking the bloodied knife in his hand. He doesn't blink as he thrusts the blade into Declan's chest. The force of it makes the man's body jolt. But it doesn't matter. The fucker's dead. Preach pierced his heart, and no doubt when he pulls it out, he'll tear an even bigger hole in his chest.

"Go shower," Ace instructs. "Mayhem, you and Storm get rid of the bodies and have Digger and Cruz help you clean this shit up."

It takes another hour before Preacher is ready. The man showered and changed his clothes. You can't tell that he just killed two people. But fuck them; they deserved what they got. The ride to the hospital is silent. We're going to have to keep our eye on Preach. The man's got a lot on his plate, and this could send him spiraling. Not to mention, his cunt of a mother has made a reappearance. That bitch wants money and Preach sends it to her. She doesn't deserve anything after what she did to the man, but he's paying what he believes is his penance. It's fucking bullshit if you ask me. He owes her nothing, and if it were me, I'd have slit her throat just as he did to Pepper.

"Mr. Collins," the nurse says when we enter the hospital floor that Tyson is on.

"Yeah?" Preach says, stepping forward.

"Tyson's stats have improved dramatically in the past two hours. He's managed to have three ounces of the bottle, and he's finally had a solid stool."

I see the relief in Ace's eyes and know that it's a good sign.

"Has the doctor seen him?" Preach asks.

The nurse nods. "He has. He's happy with how things are improving. If Tyson continues to improve, he'll be home before you know it," the nurse tells him with a smile. "She's great with him, you know." She grins. "He started to cry not long after you left, but once he was put into her arms, he settled straight away and has been content ever since."

"Thank you," Preach grunts and moves toward Tyson's room. He opens the door, and I'm rooted to the spot when I see Serenity humming gently while rocking Tyson in her arms. She looks so fucking peaceful and content in doing so. She's a natural at this.

Fuck. I want that.

I want everything with her.

ELEVEN
SERENITY

I stare down at Tyson and my heart swells. I've always wanted to be a mom; I've just wanted to get my career where I need it so that when I do eventually settle down and have children, I'll be financially stable to do so. Tyson's such a cutie, and he's so strong. I saw the pain he was in, the way he screamed, the way his body jerked. Thankfully, holding him calmed him down somewhat. It took almost an hour for him to settle and to take a bottle. The nursing staff were shocked that he took it without a fuss. They're hoping it means he's finally ready to have the milk. He's been very sporadic with his feeding. Sometimes he'll have half an ounce, other times he won't take anything.

I hear the door open, but I don't move as Tyson's on the verge of sleep, his eyes closed as he nestles against my chest. He's been silently laying in my arms for the past twenty minutes, and I've been humming as I rock him. He's such a placid little boy who is so content as he lies in my arms.

The heavy footsteps tell me Preacher's back, but also that Shadow is. Knowing he's here has my stomach filling with butterflies.

"Peach, you ready to go home?" he asks as he crouches beside me.

I lift my head and look at him. God, that gorgeous smile of his always makes my heart melt. "Yeah. Everything okay?"

"Everythin''s good," he assures me. "Let's get you home."

He reaches for Tyson, and I swear it's as though my ovaries explode as I look at him with the sweet little boy. He's so soft and gentle with him, and he's watching him with so much tenderness.

"Thank you," Preach says as he comes to help me up from the seat. "I owe you—"

I shake my head. "It was a privilege," I tell him. "Tyson is so sweet, and it's great to be able to hold a baby without one of them going for my breasts," I say pointedly, giving Ace a stern look. His twins aren't even a year old and the two of them are boob crazy. The moment they see them, they're all over them.

"Count your blessings, Seri," Preach says with a

126

laugh. "Those little heathens tried to breastfeed from Cruz last week. They got him while he was asleep. I never heard such howls comin' from the man in my life."

Shadow chuckles as he places Tyson into the crib. "Was the funniest shit I ever saw."

"They're only going to get worse," Ace sighs. "Eda's weaning them now and there's no doubt they're going to try to go elsewhere."

"As long as they stay away from mine, I'll be happy," I say with a smile. I love those little guys, but I don't need them flashing my breasts to anyone.

Shadow moves to me and wraps his arm around my neck. "Let's go," he says. "You're ready to drop."

I stick my tongue out at him. He's such a damn tattletale.

He chuckles. "Preach, we'll see you tomorrow," he says as he steers me out of the hospital room. "Do you need a pain pill?" he asks softly. "They're in my pocket."

I sink into his body. He's so darn sweet. "I'm okay," I assure him. I'm trying my hardest not to take the pain pills often.

I've seen what addiction can do to people, and that's not something that I want to happen to me. It's just so easy to slip into such a heavy addiction without even realizing you've become an addict.

When Esme and I were at college, a friend of ours

was at college on a scholarship. She was an amazing athlete. She ran track, but one day, she was heavily injured. The pain pills she took were there to help her manage her day-to-day life as it was excruciating for her to walk, since she tore her achilles. Within a month, she was addicted. It hit her hard, and she ended up dropping out. The last I heard, she was still struggling with getting clean.

"If you need it, Peach, let me know," he says, watching me carefully.

"I'm good, honestly. I spent the past few hours sitting with a baby in my arms. It's the perfect medicine. Besides, we have a date tonight."

He grins wide. "That we do, Peach. That we do."

Before we leave the hospital, I make a pit stop and grab Preacher some food. The man looks as though he hasn't eaten since Tyson was born. Ace runs it to his room while Shadow and I go out to the car.

"Is she dead?" I ask softly, unsure if he'll answer the question.

He pulls me to a stop just beside the truck. "Serenity, I get that you're new to this world, and I'll do everythin' in my power to shield you from it. The violence and shit that I do doesn't touch you. Not fuckin' ever."

"I love that," I whisper. "My daddy loves me, Shadow. He adores us and our mom. I've always wanted that, but I never found a man who would care for me the way my dad does my mom. Until you."

His eyes darken and his nostrils flare. "Always," he growls, the word vibrating in his chest. "Never fuckin' doubt just how much I fuckin' adore you."

"You're going to make me fall for you," I whisper, knowing that I've already started to fall.

His hand curls around my neck and he pulls me closer. "Good," he says. "I want everythin' with you, Serenity. I want you in my life and my bed. Not just for a short time for some fun. But forever."

I want that. I really want that. But I can't help but feel that it's moving so fast.

He doesn't give me a chance to answer. His lips press against mine, and once again he takes everything with just one kiss, leaving me breathless and wanting more.

"You're hesitant," he tells me. "That's okay, baby. We'll get you there."

I narrow my eyes. "You mean muddle my brain?"

That cocky grin of his forms, and I roll my eyes. "You're determined," I sigh.

He nods. "I am, and you're stubborn," he counters.

I laugh. I can't deny that. I am stubborn, but there's a reason as to why I am, and that's so I don't rush into this and get hurt. But I'm giving him everything that I can.

Ace arrives and our conversation is cut short. Shadow helps me into the vehicle and climbs into the driver's seat while Ace hops into the passenger's. I close my eyes as the two of them start to talk.

I WAKE when I'm jostled. Blinking, I notice I'm lying on a bed, and I'm in Shadow's room.

"Hey," I say groggily. "I'm sorry I fell asleep."

He shrugs as he helps me into a sitting position. "You're fine, Peach. You needed the sleep. Your body's still recoverin'."

I glance around the room and do a double take. "How long was I out for?" I ask, noticing there's a TV on the dresser, which is now pushed against the wall opposite the bed. Not to mention there's two pizza boxes at the bottom of the bed.

He chuckles. "You needed the sleep. I sent Ace to the store to get a TV. Your laptop's the shit, babe, but I ain't watchin' a movie on that screen. Besides, once a week, we're havin' movie night."

I blink. "We are?"

His tongue flicks the ring piercing on his lip. "Bein' in a room with you alone? Fuck yeah, that's what we're doin'. Now, you ready to eat?"

I nod just as my stomach starts to rumble. My cheeks heat and Shadow chuckles. He leans forward and pulls the pizza boxes toward him.

"Tell me about your family," he says, and I'm surprised but amazed that he's taking the time to get to know me.

"Octavia is my best friend, but don't tell Esme that," I say with a smile. "My mom and dad are amazing. They can be a little over the top with how they act, but we get it, especially with what happened between Octavia and River." I pause and swallow hard. "Do you know about that?"

His eyes are soft as he looks at me. "Yeah, Peach, I know. You don't have to relive it."

I'm grateful. It's hard. I hate talking about it. The last time I did, I was drunk and spilled everything to Kinsley as she was worried about Octavia. After ripping open all those wounds, I couldn't sleep properly. I was so scared that River would come back and hurt her.

"It was really hard watching as she tried to hide what really happened after the surgery. She tried to hide the fact that she couldn't see properly." I shake my head. The pain of that date still haunts me. "She thought she was paying a penance, that she deserved to be partially blind for letting him into her life."

"Christ," he growls.

"So I get their overprotection and the way they close ranks when something happens. My brothers are worse," I say with a sigh. "I'm not sure why I haven't heard from them. It's unlike them." All three of them are usually up in my business, demanding to know what I'm doing and where I'm going, and now, nothing. Not even a text message.

"They've been checkin' up on you," he says, and I frown. "They call Tavia every day, probably twice a day."

Ah. That makes sense. My parents have been doing the same. I've spoken to my mom and dad while I've been here, but they haven't been continuously on my case like I had assumed they would.

"I love my family, and I know that I'm lucky to have them. What about you? Do you have any?" I ask softly, knowing that family can be a touchy subject for some people.

He settles back against the bed and reaches for the pizza. I follow suit and see that he's got me a cheese and pepperoni. I'm a classic girl when it comes to food.

"Thank you," I say as I begin to tuck into the pizza. "You don't have to tell me. I understand. How did you become part of the Fury Vipers?"

He grins. "That's easy. That's down to Storm. He's more than a brother to me. We've been friends since we were kids. When he told me he was joinin',

132

that this was what he wanted, the way he spoke about it, I knew I had to see what he was talking about for myself. And he wasn't lyin'. This is family right here, Seri."

My heart melts. "That's the first time you've called me that."

His brows furrow. "What?"

"Seri. You usually call me Serenity, babe, baby, or Peach, but never Seri." He shrugs at my words. "Will you tell me what your real name is?"

"Graham," he says as he continues to eat.

"I like it," I say. It suits him. But then again, Shadow does too. The man needs a bell on him. He sneaks up behind you. The amount of times he's scared me, it's a wonder the man hasn't given someone heart failure.

"That's good, Peach. You're the only one who's allowed to call me that," he says, unfazed as he continues to eat, not realizing that he's just completely knocked me for six.

I stare at him. God, there's no doubt about it any longer. I'm so far gone that I can't even see the line any longer.

Oh my. I'm in love with him.

TWELVE
SHADOW

I never thought I could stun her like I did by telling her only she's allowed to call me Graham. But she's looking at me with big eyes and a soft expression. "You good?" I ask her, knowing if I made a big deal about it, she'll freak.

She blinks a few times and gives me a beaming smile. "I'm good. So tell me about your life," she breathes as she leans closer to me. "I now know that you and Storm are tighter than I expected. I love that for you. What else don't I know?"

I have no idea what switched in her today, but I'm fucking glad it did. "I build custom bikes. It's what this club does. We own a custom ride business. Whether it be bikes or cars."

"That's awesome. Did you do your own?" she asks, finally starting to eat again.

I've seen her looking at my bike. "I did. You like it?"

She grins. "It's amazing. I've never been on one before."

"That's a fuckin' damn shame, Peach. Having you straddlin' my bike is goin' to be a memory I'll never forget."

Her cheeks flame but she doesn't hide away. "When I'm better, maybe we can go for a ride?"

Fuck, there's a double meaning to her words, and fuck yes, I'll fuck her on my bike. I love that she's up for anything. "Without a fuckin' doubt, babe."

"Are you from New York, originally?"

I nod. "The outskirts. Dansville."

She tilts her head. "I've never been."

Good. I would never bring her there. That shit's in my past and I have no intention of ever going back.

"Do you love to travel?" she asks. She's just firing question after question. I fucking love that she's doing this, that she's taking the time to get to know me after I gave her the opening.

"I do. There's nothing better than bein' on my bike with an open road in front of me. What about you?"

She nods. "I love traveling. Octavia and I went traveling around Europe a few years ago. We managed to visit six countries. My dream is to travel to all fifty states before I die."

Fuck. Can she get any better?

I'll make her dream come true. Little does she know that's exactly what I planned to do, too. It's on my kick-it list. "Tell you what, baby, your dream is goin' to become a reality. We're goin' to do it on the back of my bike."

"Graham," she whimpers, and my cock thickens. I've tried to be a gentleman, to keep control of my impulses, but hearing her whimper and that soft as fuck sweet moan, I can't hold back any longer.

"I hope you like cold pizza, babe," I tell her as I reach for the boxes and move them to the floor. "I'm goin' to fuck you now, baby."

Her breathing becomes choppy, and her eyes fill with heat and want. "Graham," she whispers. "I need you."

I move, needing to taste her. I position myself over her. "Gonna let you know, babe, that I'm clean. I got tested and haven't been with anyone since I was."

She swallows. "I'm clean too. I'm also on the pill."

Fuck yes.

I press my lips against hers, and she doesn't hold back. She opens her mouth, giving me what I want.

My tongue slides in and the kiss turns frenzied. She whimpers again, and my cock thickens even more.

It's hot, hard, and heavy. Never have I wanted anyone as much as I want her. It's always been her. I was just too fucking consumed by the past to understand that.

I slide my hand down her body until I reach her panties. She's wearing a sweet as fuck dress that gives me the perfect access. I push aside her panties and sink a finger into her hot, wet channel.

Fuck, I forgot how fucking good her pussy felt. So fucking tight. I finger-fuck her, dying to hear the sound of her coming. It's not long before she's grinding against my finger.

I pull back from the kiss and move down her body. I loop my finger into her panties and tear them from her body. She opens her legs, giving me the access I need to taste her. I run my tongue along her slit.

She groans low and hard as I fuck her with my tongue. There's absolutely no finesse with this at all. It's hard and fast, pushing her close to her limit. She's soaked. Fucking drenched. And she's mewling like a damn cat.

Her thighs quake as I continue to tongue-fuck her. I'm not stopping until she detonates. Her movements are a little jerky, but her head's thrown back while she grinds harder against my mouth. It doesn't take much for her to topple over the edge. She screams out my name as her juices flood my tongue.

Fuck, she tastes so fucking good. My cock is aching, pressed against my zipper. I need to fuck her. I pull back while she's still reeling from her orgasm and strip out of my clothes. My cock springs free, and I see that it's leaking pre-cum.

I position myself over her and slide into her. I groan deep at the tightness of her. Fuck, I forgot how fucking good it was to be inside of her. Nothing compares to this. Shit, it was nowhere near what I remembered. I capture her lips, tasting her, dominating her. Our tongues tangle together. I can't get enough of her. I never will. I wasted five years of being without her.

She wraps an arm around my neck, the one in a cast resting on the bed. "Graham," she whimpers. "Please."

I rotate my hips and fuck her harder. I feel the tingles on my spine. I'm close. It's been too fucking long since I had her. Not to mention, I'm fucking her bareback. Nothing has felt this damn good. Ever. I hammer into her like a man possessed. Every stroke is fast and frenzied, but I hit her deep.

"Yes," she gasps. "Right there. Oh, Graham, please," she cries.

I fuck her harder, my balls swelling. I'm about

ready to burst. Her pussy walls tighten around me, her body shakes, and she cries out my name. I slip over the edge, unable to hold back. I thrust deep once more and bury myself inside of her, groaning as I come.

I bury my head in the crook of her neck. We're both sweaty and our breathing is ragged. She starts to giggle, and my cock dislodges from her pussy. "What the fuck, Peach?"

She snorts as she laughs, and I look down at her and see that she's in a fit of giggles.

"Sorry," she breathes as she winces. "There's something under my ass and I'm pretty sure it's garlic bread."

I drop down beside her, pulling her with me, and see that she's right. The box of garlic bread I got is now squashed to hell, and I'm pretty sure it's covered in our juices. I get to my feet with her in my arms and carry her to the bathroom. "Shower, babe."

"Your cum's leaking down my thigh." She sighs as she rests her head against my shoulder. "After the shower, can I have one of the pain pills?"

"I'll get it for you now," I tell her as I set her down on the counter by the sink. She shakes her head and tells me about her friend who got addicted to them. She doesn't want the same thing to happen to her. I respect that but fucking hate that she's not taking the damn pills when she's in pain. I don't want her suffering when she should be healing. But I'm not going to pressure her to take the damn things. She has her reasons and I'm going to respect them.

"Just promise if it gets too bad, you'll take the pill?" I ask as I switch the shower on.

She nods as she reaches for the plastic wrapping I have for her when she needs to shower. It takes us a while to get her cast wrapped, but the moment it's done, I pull her into the shower and start to wash her.

"I can do it," she says, her voice soft.

"You can, but I'm doin' it," I say, and I love that she doesn't fight me on it. She leans against me and lets me take care of her.

Forty minutes later, we're dressed and sitting on the bed, choosing which movie to watch.

"No horrors," she says, trying to reach for the TV remote. I wrap my arm around her waist and pull her closer to me.

"You scared, baby?" I ask with a grin. "I'll protect you."

She elbows me. "No, I've just seen enough shit to last a lifetime."

"No horror movies, Peach. What about *Die Hard*?"

She pauses for a moment. "I've never seen it," she confesses. "Is it good?"

"It is, so settle down, eat, and watch," I tell her as I get the movie started.

She leans her head against my shoulder, her eyes bright as she looks up at me. "Thank you," she whispers. "For wanting this. I never thought I could be this happy and yet you make it so effortlessly."

Fuck. This woman is killing me.

"Keep that up. Babe, and I swear I'll be balls deep inside of you in a second. You're in pain and I don't want to add to it. Be a good girl."

She grins as she reaches for a pizza slice.

"But you gotta know, Seri, that nothing is as easy as bein' with you. I fuckin' love that, and I'm goin' to enjoy every day of the rest of our lives."

"Sweet talker," she says and turns to face the TV.

We're both skirting around the word love. I fucking love her. There's absolutely no denying it. And I know she feels the same. I can see it every time she looks at me. Is it too soon? No, it's been five years in the making. I'm not stupid; I know I fell for her that night we spent together. It's just taken us this long to get this together. Now I have her, I'm not losing her.

Twenty minutes into the movie and there's a knock at the door. Storm walks in after I shout for him to enter.

"Yo, Prez said you got a TV and are watchin'

movies. What the fuck, bro? You hidin' your girl from the rest of us?"

I nod. "Too fuckin' right I am. You're an ass who won't stop hittin' on her. So fuck yes, I'm keepin' her out of your reach."

I smile as the fucker helps himself to the discarded garlic bread at the foot of the bed. "You eatin' these?" he questions as he takes a bite.

"Nope, all yours, bro. But I'm watchin' a movie with my woman, so see yourself out."

The fucker grins as he carries the squashed box of food out of my room.

"You can't let him eat that," Serenity says, horrified.

"I fuckin' can. The fucker wanted to be nosey and greedy; he gets what's comin' to him."

She shakes her head but continues to eat. "This movie is great. You chose good. I may even let you choose next week."

"Cute, babe, but I'm not watchin' any fuckin' romcoms or stupid lovey dovey shit."

"Hey," she says, affronted.

"What's your favorite movie, Peach?"

She scowls at me. "You're an ass, Graham. I have an eclectic taste. I like comedies, such as *The Hangover*. Action too, like *Fast and Furious* or *Taken*. As for romance, I like *The Notebook*."

"Some of those movies are the shit, babe. We can watch them. I'm never watchin' *The Notebook*."

She rolls her eyes at me. "We'll see," she replies, turning her gaze back to the TV.

This is what I've been missing. Just shooting the shit with her. We used to do it whenever she was around the clubhouse. But after we slept together, she never came around me. I get it, it fucking sucked, but now I have it back.

THIRTEEN

SERENITY

"You can't be serious?" I ask Graham incredulously.

He crosses his arms over his chest and glares at me.

I sigh. These past couple of weeks have been amazing. Graham and I have become so much closer, more than I could have ever hoped. I still don't know about his family, but I'm hoping he'll open up about it when he feels ready. But he's become protective, even more so than my brothers are, and right now, he's being overprotective.

"Graham, seriously," I say. "You've got work to do. I have classes that I have to take." I've tried my hardest to keep up with the workload. Missing my actual job, along with not being able to attend college, has been hard for me. I'm an overachiever;

I'm not afraid to admit it. I also know that my anxiety will spike if I don't get back to normal soon. I can visualize everything piling on top of me, and sooner or later, I'm going to be buried beneath it all.

"Peach, we're not arguin'," he says, stepping into my space. "You think that I'm goin' to let my woman be out in public alone, with the cunts who hurt you walkin' free? Think again, baby, 'cause that's never goin' to happen."

The way his jaw is set, along with the determination in his eyes, tells me he's not budging on this. I know that me getting hurt was a huge trigger for him. It spurred something inside of him. Octavia and Effie told me I need to pick my battles.

"Are you going to be attending my classes too?" I ask, hoping that he won't because there's no way I'll be able to concentrate with him beside me.

His grin tells me he knows exactly what I'm thinking. "No, Peach, I'll be waitin' outside. I'll make sure no one gets near you."

"Okay, I won't argue. I know this is something you need to do. I finish at three. I'm not working until next week. Would you prefer it if I come to the auto shop with you after and study there?" He's not working, no matter how often I tell him I'm safe at the clubhouse. It's as though he doesn't want to be apart from me. And I get it, he's worried, but he has a job to do and I hate that I'm the one who's keeping him from it.

"Yeah, babe, that'll be good. You can study in the office," he tells me. "If there's anythin' you need, let me know and I'll have one of the guys bring it over for you," he says, his brown eyes soft and filled with emotion.

"I'll have everything with me. Maybe we can stop for snacks on the way?"

He shakes his head and chuckles. "You need snacks to study?"

I roll my eyes. "Yes, of course. It's a cardinal sin not to have them. How else are you supposed to feed your brain while it takes in all the information?"

"Get your shit, babe. We're leavin' in five," he says, shaking his head. "I gotta speak to Ace, but I'll meet you at the car."

I can't help but pout. "You're not taking your bike?"

Heat fills his eyes, turning them from brown to almost black. "You still haven't recovered, Seri. I put you on the back of my bike now and you'll be sore. Once your ribs are better, we'll take a ride," he promises me. I open my mouth to speak, but he beats me. "Don't tell me they're fine. I know you're lyin'. I can tell every time you laugh or move in a certain way they hurt. So, no, we're not goin' today."

I hold my hands up and back away. I can't keep the smile off my face. "Fine, whatever you say."

"Exactly, baby, whatever I say, so tonight, you're on your knees, takin' my cock between those luscious lips."

Heat pools between my thighs. "Yes, sir," I breathe as I salute him.

His grin is sexy as hell. "Go," he growls. "Before I take you back upstairs, tie you to the bed, and fuck you until you pass out."

I move quickly. As much as I'd love for him to do that to me, I'm not going to miss any more days. I'm already behind.

"Seri," Effie says as I walk up the stairs. "I'm impressed. It's been two weeks and you've already got him figured out."

I blink. "What do you mean?" I ask, wondering what she's talking about.

"Shadow." She beams at me. "He was all set for an argument, but you let him tell you why he needed it and then you relented and even had him promising sex later. It took me and Octavia a while to figure out how to do that."

I shrug. "If I can stop us from arguing and alleviate his fear, then I'll do that. But I won't be strongarmed into doing anything. As you and Tavia said, I should pick my battles, and having him sit outside the college isn't something I'm going to argue with."

"You're worried," she surmises. "Do you think Shadow knows that?"

I sigh. "Probably, although he hasn't mentioned it. But yeah, the men knew where I lived. It wouldn't take a genius to know where I work or go to college."

"You'll be fine," she assures me. "Just don't go anywhere alone and make sure you're with someone at all times until Shadow can get to you." She pulls me into her arms and holds me tight. "Call me if you're walking and need someone to talk to."

My heart swells at her words. I do that a lot when I'm walking alone at night. I always call my mom, dad, or Tavia. If I were to call my brothers, they'd demand that I go inside the nearest store and wait for them to come and get me. Thankfully, my parents aren't as crazy and they talk to me, while the other is nearby with their keys in hand. Knowing that Effie knows what I do makes my heart warm.

"Thanks, Ef."

"Hey, this is what sisters do. If our positions were reversed, you'd do the same," she says. "Although, don't tell Shadow that you walk alone at night. I think that'll send him over the edge."

I can't help but laugh. She's right, I think he'd have an aneurysm if I told him that. I understand the dangers of walking alone at night, but sometimes it can't be helped. Usually, it's me walking to my car from work or college. It's such a scary world that we live in. Even though I may be safe, I don't feel it when I'm alone.

"I've got to go," I tell her as I reach the room I'm sharing with Graham. "I'll call you if I'm alone, and if you're bored, tell Octavia that you think you saw a scuff mark on the floor. It's funny to watch as she tries to find it. I think Ruby and I have done it to her five times this week alone and she falls for it every single time."

My sister and I are complete opposites. She's a neat freak, whereas I will tidy up whenever I get around to it. I'm not dirty by any means, I'm just not Octavia. She's gotten worse since she gave birth to Serafina, making sure that everything is clean and there's not a single cup out of place. It's neurotic, but cleaning makes her happy.

Effiemia grins. "Oh, I do something similar. I tell her that I see a gray hair, and it sends her crazy when she can't find one."

I smile. Oh, now I have something else to annoy her with. "You know, when she finds out what we're doing, she's going to kill us," I tell her as I grab my backpack from the room.

Effie shrugs. "It's worth it. I love Tavia, and she'll pay us back tenfold."

"I'll look forward to it," I say, knowing that once my sister gets going, her revenge is going to be sweet. "Did you know that Sera and Ruby have been asking for a dog?" I say as we start to make our way back downstairs.

"They have, have they? Well, well, their birthdays are coming up soon. Wouldn't it be a great present to get them?" she says. Both Effie and I adore our nieces and nephews. We'll do anything to make them happy, and both girls have wanted a dog for a while now.

I nod. I agree, it would make a great present. "Elouise wants one too. We should get one for the clubhouse. That way, it's not all down to one couple to look after."

Effie pulls me to a stop and smiles. "Then we need to talk with the women and get them to work on the men. If anyone can get those men to agree, it's us."

Oh, that's for sure. The old ladies know how to work the men and get them to agree with them.

"If we're going to do this, then we need to agree to let the men decide on the dog and tell them that it's added protection."

She snaps her fingers. "That's it. God, Seri, you're a genius."

"Okay, you talk to the girls while I work on Graham. Hopefully, by the end of the day, we'll have the men agreeing."

Her smile is bright and filled with hope. If the men agree, the kids are all going to be happy.

They've wanted a pet for a while and a dog is at the top of their list.

IT'S BEEN A LONG DAY. I'm sore, and my brain is fuzzy. I'm not as behind as I had thought, but it was too much. I'm still not at my best, and I should have taken another few days to recover. My body is exhausted and I'm about ready to drop. Thankfully, this class is almost finished.

I send Graham a message, letting him know that I should be out within the next ten minutes. I have no doubt that as soon as he starts to drive, I'm going to be fast asleep. I'm that damn zonked.

Once the class finishes, I pack up my bag and start to walk toward the exit. Every step I take is painful, the movement sore on my ribs, but I grit my teeth and push through. I'll take a pill when I get to the car. Knowing Graham, he has them in his pocket.

"Serenity," I hear called out as I walk outside.

My heart starts to race as I recognize the voice. My gaze moves around the crowd of people in search of Graham, but there's just so many people that I can't see clearly.

A hand clamps around my arm, and I turn to see Eric. Fuck. I should have kept walking.

"Take your hands off me," I hiss at him, trying to wrench my arm free.

"Where the fuck have you been?" he snarls at me. "I go to your house and you're not there. Your car is but you're not. So what the fuck gives?"

"Why were you at my house?" I ask, dread settling in my stomach. What does he want?

"You're hurt and you didn't call me?"

I stare at him in absolute horror. "Why on earth would I do that? We've not been together in over six weeks, Eric. You shouldn't be at my house."

His grip tightens on my arm. "I was giving you space," he growls. "Time for you to realize that you want me, want us. But you're such a stuck-up bitch, Serenity. No wonder you got worked over."

I try once again to wrench my arm from him, but it's no use. His grip is tight, and he's not letting go.

"I would never get back with you," I say, my hand clawing at his to get off me. "You're the reason I was worked over, asshole. You owe people money, and you're such a fucking douchebag that you gave them my address."

I see that I was right when his nostrils flare and anger enters his eyes. "Cunt," he growls. "You should have just given them the money."

"Go to hell. I am not your fucking mother. Then again, she didn't want you either. Get your fucking hands off me."

He pulls me toward him, and fear works its way up my throat.

"You heard her." I hear the angry snarl from Shadow, and relief washes through me.

He's here.

.

FOURTEEN
SHADOW

"Your woman talk to you about this fuckin' dog?" Ace growls.

I pull my cell from my ear and smirk. Yeah, I know all about the damn dog. I also know it's Serenity and Effiemia's idea. The women want their nieces to be happy and the girls have been wanting a mutt for a long time. Having a club dog isn't a bad idea, not if we can get a trained guard dog. It'll protect the women and children and it'll make the kids happy. I'm all for it.

"She did," I say, bringing my cell back to my ear. "But you and I both know, Prez, that if you don't okay it, it's not happenin'."

I hear his sigh. No doubt he's running his hand through his hair. The man is going to be bald by the time he's forty if he keeps that shit up. Then again, with his two little heathens, it wouldn't surprise anyone if he lost his hair by then.

"All of the women are in this shit together. Now they've got the kids askin'. Fuck, even the twins are at it."

I grin out the windshield. There's no way he's going to deny his boys anything. Hell, the man can't say no to his woman.

"So, when are you gettin' the dog?"

"Asshole," he grunts. "I've made a few calls. There's two for sale that I could pick up by the weekend."

The man wants this too. There's no way he's putting all that effort in right away if he doesn't want it. "Okay, how much and what breed?"

"Bullmastiffs, and they're pricey. You're lookin' at three thousand dollars per pup, and those fuckers aren't even trained yet. But the parents are and they're selling the entire litter. Mom, Dad, and three pups."

"Fuck, bro, the girls wanted one dog, not an entire fuckin' pound."

"I'm not havin' arguments. This way, there is none. I'm sending Storm and Cruz to go get them. Digger and Raptor are goin' to get everythin' we need. The dogs will be here by the end of the week."

Fuck. He's gone all in. The women will be happy, that's for sure. Although, I'd say they'd be surprised that he went with Bullmastiffs rather than something a little less terrifying.

I spot Serenity walking out of the college, and I can see that she's in pain. Fuck. It was too early for her to go back. She should have waited another week. I climb out of the vehicle, Ace still talking about the damn dogs and what we're going to do with them.

I start to move toward her, when I see a fucking bastard put his hands on her. I instantly know it's Eric. He's going to die for touching her.

"I gotta go," I snarl. "Fuckin' Eric's here."

"I'm sendin' two brothers to you. Try not to kill him. The last thing we need is for you to be on the run too."

"I won't kill him in broad daylight," I tell him. "But make the brothers hurry." I end the call and move quickly. That fucker is going to be in for a world of hurt.

"I was giving you space," the fucking prick says to her. "Time for you to realize that you want me, want us. But you're such a stuck-up bitch, Serenity. No wonder you got worked over."

Oh, he really needs to be taught a lesson. He shouldn't be anywhere fucking near her.

"I would never get back with you," she spits at him. "You're the reason I was worked over, asshole.

You owe people money, and you're such a fucking douchebag that you gave them my address."

"Cunt," he growls. "You should have just given them the money."

"Go to hell. I am not your fucking mother. Then again, she didn't want you either. Get your fucking hands off me."

I would smile at her feistiness, but that fucking prick pulls her toward him.

"You heard her," I snarl at him. "Take your fuckin' hands off her."

He glances at me, his eyes widening a fraction before narrowing. "You fucking him now?" he hisses at her. "You're a fucking whore, Serenity."

The cunt releases her, and I'm able to breathe somewhat.

"Yeah, well you're a fucking dildo, asshole. When a woman tells you not to touch her, don't fucking touch her."

"A biker, Serenity? You sure love slumming it, don't you?"

I've heard all the insults before. People assume that we're stupid, poor, and the lowest of the low. But we'd never let a woman pay for our sins like this cunt did.

"Slumming it?" she snaps at him. "Hell no. Shadow's little finger is more of a man than you are. But let's face it, you're jealous. One: he's so much hotter than you. Two: he treats me like a lady. Three: he cares about me and isn't afraid to show it. And four: the man can make me come. You could use a few pointers."

Hearing her talk about her sexual experience with him has me gritting my teeth. Fuck, I hate it. I'm not stupid; I know she's been with others, but fuck, I don't need to hear it. Though it's a relief knowing the bastard's shit in the sack.

"Always such a bitch," he growls. "Don't worry, man," he says to me. "She'll end it soon enough. Serenity doesn't let anyone get too close. She's so focused on her career."

I wrap my arm around her waist and pull her into me. She looks as though she's ready to launch herself at him and try to beat the shit out of him.

"Funny," I murmur. "It's my bed she's been in for the past two weeks. She's my woman, man, and all you're doin' is showin' how fuckin' stupid you were to let her go."

Seri reaches out and touches my chest. "Uh, no. I dumped him. He wanted more, but I didn't want it with him. I've worked my ass off to be where I am today and I'm not giving up my dreams. He wanted me to become a housewife, and I'm not down with that."

I've known this woman for five years. I know how damn hard she's worked to get where she is. I'm fucking proud of her. There's no way I'm going to let her give up what she loves. Hell, I'm going to get her to make new dreams once she's achieved her Masters. Keep her reaching for the stars.

"So what—you're living with him?"

"What's it to you?" I demand.

"She was mine," he growls. "I'm not giving her up."

"She was yours," I counter, stepping forward and pulling Seri behind me. "She dumped your sorry fuckin' ass, and I wised the fuck up and realized that she's mine. I'm not lettin' her go, and man, I'll fuckin' kill to protect her. You put your hands on her, and you fucked up by letting those fucking cunts hurt her."

His jaw clenches.

"Who were they?" I demand. "Why the fuck did you tell them she would pay your debts?"

He's jumpy, looking from side to side. He's not going to tell me. Stupid fucking cunt. I hear the rumble of pipes in the distance and know that my brothers are here.

"There's nowhere for you to hide, Eric. You're goin' to tell us one way or another. Who do you owe money to?"

"I'm not talking to you, asshole," he snarls. "Just because you're fucking her now, it doesn't mean shit. You're not the first and I doubt you'll be the last."

I see Ace, Digger, and Mayhem moving toward us, and none of them look happy. Then again, Seri's their sister, and this bastard is the reason she was beaten. None of us are feeling anything but rage toward the fucking prick.

"Funny," Seri says, her hand pressed against my back. Thankfully, she moves to my side rather than to my front. "You stand there and act as though you have any clue about me. We had three dates. Three. We fucked twice, and it was shit. The second time I don't even remember because I was black-out drunk. So you have no fucking idea about what I want."

A red haze forms over me. That motherfucker fucked her while she was unable to tell the cunt no.

Mayhem moves behind Eric and curls his hand into his shoulder. I smirk when the fucker winces in pain. Good, because he's in for a world of hurt.

"You're goin' with him," I say, loving the fear that enters his eyes.

We watch as Digger and Mayhem drag the fucker to the van. Serenity stays at my side, her body pressed against mine. She's about ready to fall.

"Take her home, brother," Ace instructs. "She's not goin' to last standin' much longer. You'll get to dole out your punishment. We're not goin' to let anyone else do it."

I nod, grateful that my brothers have my back. "See you at the clubhouse," I tell him as I wrap my arm around Serenity's shoulders. She presses closer against me. "Come on, Peach, let's get you into the truck and get you a pain pill."

She nods against my shoulder but doesn't utter a word.

Once we're in the truck and she's taken a pill, I turn to her. "Babe, we've got to talk," I say as I start the engine.

"Hmm?" she says, her eyes fuzzy, and I know she's fighting against herself to sleep. "What's wrong?"

"I know you and your girls go out and party, but do you get black-out drunk often?"

She shakes her head. "Never," she says. "I swear, Graham, it only happened that one time, and fuck, I can't even remember what happened that night. I woke up the next morning and Kale was on my couch. He said he wanted to check in with me. I said I was fine, and he left. Eric turned up thirty minutes later, wearing the same clothes as the night before, and he had coffee and food. He told me what happened."

I grit my teeth. That asshole is going to die, painfully and slowly.

"I don't know what happened," she whispers, and I reach over and take her hand. "I don't drink heavily. I can, but I hate throwing up, so I don't." She turns to me, a soft look in her eyes. "It took a while for me to go out again after that," she confesses. "I don't want to be like that again."

"You go out, babe, but you do it when I'm around you. You want to get drunk, go for it. I'll make sure you're okay."

"Graham," she whispers. "I love you, I really do, but I'm so damn scared I'll get hurt."

I pull the car over and reach for her, unbuckling her seatbelt and pulling her into my lap. The moment she's settled, I frame her face. "I love you, Serenity Michaels. Never fuckin' doubt that."

Tears well in her eyes. "You do?"

"Yes," I growl, the sound echoing in my chest. "So fuckin' much. Christ, baby, I never thought I'd find my old lady."

"Stop," she says as she grips my tee. "God, Graham, you're making me cry."

"Don't," I say, hating that she's fucking shedding a single drop. "I can't fuckin' bear seeing you cry."

She smiles. "They're happy tears, I promise."

I take her mouth, needing to taste her. I tangle my hand into her hair, sweeping my tongue into her mouth, and take everything from her. I reluctantly pull away, when in fact all I want to do is fuck her and show her how much I love her.

"Into your seat, baby," I instruct her. "We'll get you home and you can sleep."

"Okay, handsome," she whispers as she pulls her seatbelt around her.

Fuck. It feels so fucking good to finally tell her how I feel. Knowing that she feels the same is like a weight lifting off my chest. For the past five years, a tightness was there, but now it's gone.

Finally, I have my old lady.

FIFTEEN
SHADOW

"You good?" May asks Serenity as soon as we enter the clubhouse.

She nods, giving him a soft smile. "I'm good. He didn't hurt me."

So she says, but that fuck had his hands on her and that's enough for me to lose my mind. Fuck, having that prick so fucking close to her was more than I could bear. It took every ounce of restraint that I had not to smash my fist into his face. The fucker just kept his mouth running. Christ, the shit he was spewing... He's never going to get the message that Serenity isn't his, and that's another reason he's going to die.

"Did he give up who the fuck he owes money to?" Digger questions.

She shakes her head. "No. The dildo just wanted to try and stake his claim on me."

That's twice she's called him a dildo.

Digger releases a heavy sigh. "You've been listening to Octavia," he says.

"Hey," the woman in question says, affronted. "But no, we all know what that means."

Effie nods. "Yep."

I glance around at my brothers and see their blank expressions. At least I'm not the only one who has no idea what the fuck they're talking about.

"Maybe you could enlighten us?" I ask with a raised brow.

Serenity smiles, her hand sliding around my stomach. "Calling someone a dildo is a better insult than calling someone a dick," she says, her smile bright. "Basically, it's saying they're not real enough to be a dick. Or in Eric's case, not man enough to know how to use it."

I chuckle. I have no idea where the hell these women get their shit from, but I can't fucking argue with it.

"Peach, go to bed and sleep," I tell her as I press a kiss against her lips. "You need to rest. I'll wake you when I'm back and we can have dinner and you can study, okay?"

"You need to work," she sighs. "I'm sorry, Graham, I'm making things worse for you."

172

I frame her face. "No, you're not. Told you already, babe: I fuckin' love you. Work will always be there. I need you safe, yeah?"

She nods, her eyes soft and her expression filled with love. "Yeah. Be safe," she tells me.

Fuck. Yeah, my life with her in it is going to be fucking amazing.

The moment she steps out of my embrace, she's surrounded by Effie and Octavia. She's safe here and she has her sisters. No matter what, she's going to be okay. Her bruising will fade and so will the memories of what happened. It's just going to take time.

I pull out my cell and turn on my heel. I have a call to make before I go and see Eric.

"Yo, you good?" Malice answers.

I hear footsteps behind me, but I don't need to turn. I already know it's Digger and Mayhem. Hell, I wouldn't be surprised if Ace is with them.

"I am, but I need some answers, and from what I can gather, you're the man who'll answer them."

"Shoot," he says without missing a beat.

"Serenity told me that she went out one night and can't remember what happened, but she woke with you in her house—"

"Nothin' happened, man," he says, cutting me off. "She was in Utopia," he says through clenched teeth. The club is known for its drug use. Many women have been roofied while there. "I was meetin' someone, but when I spotted Seri—alone, I may add—I got a fuckin' weird feelin'. I had one of my boys bring the woman I was meetin' home and stayed with Seri."

I fucking appreciate that he was watching out for her. "You spoke to her that night?"

"Yeah. Whenever I meet the girls in the club, I always make a point to go over and speak with them. It sends a message to anyone in there that they're not to be touched," he says with a bite to his tone.

My respect for the man has gone up since we found out that he knew what was happening to Kinsley. While no one touched him because he was with her throughout her darkest times, it didn't stop us all from hating the fucker. But with each woman that my brothers have fallen for, Kale seems to be involved in their lives in one way or another. Being Effiemia's brother, it means he's involved in hers, Octavia's, and Serenity's more than the others. Malice views all three women as his sisters and will do whatever the fuck it takes to protect them.

"She said she got black-out drunk. But from what she told me, that doesn't seem to ring true—"

"It's not," he says, cutting me off once again. "I watched her enter that club, Shadow. I fuckin' kept an eye on her. She had no more than three drinks and she was all over the place. Her speech was slurred, and she was fucking stumblin' around that club. I'm tellin' you, man, I've watched Seri drink men under the table and be fine. That wasn't the effects of alcohol."

I grit my teeth. She was drugged. I fucking knew the situation wasn't as it seemed.

"Did that cunt Eric get a hold of her?" I snarl. I have no doubt that it was him who drugged her. Fucking bastard thought it was the only way he could have her.

"Is she around you?" he asks, his voice rumbling with anger.

"No. I have Eric, and I'm about to interrogate him. The fucker set her up to be beaten, and I'm goin' to enjoy returnin' the favor."

"What?" he hisses. "Want to repeat that?"

I still, my hand going to my nape. "You didn't know?" I ask, my gaze sliding to Mayhem. Usually, Effie tells him everything. If it's not her, it's Tavia. Hell, even Kinsley does.

"No," he growls. "I'm on my way. There's a fuck of a lot that you don't know about that night, and Shadow, when you find out, you're goin' to lay even more hurt on the cunt. The only reason I didn't was 'cause he fuckin' ran the next mornin' and no one saw him after that."

My jaw locks. Hence why those fucking bastards worked over Serenity. They thought by hurting her, they'd pull him out of hiding. It worked. Fuck.

"Get your ass here," I tell him and end the call.

"What happened?" Digger asks. "What did he tell you?"

"He's on his way," I tell them. "No one told him what happened with Seri, and he's beyond pissed." I tell them about what was said about the night in the club, knowing that they both overheard what Serenity said to the cunt.

"I fuckin' knew there was somethin' more," Mayhem snarls. "I've known Serenity for as long as I can remember. She likes to party, but she's sensible about it. She's got a level head but loves to annoy the shit out of people—'specially Octavia—but she'd never put her, her girls, or anyone, for that matter, in danger. She's always conscious about what she drinks. The woman is fuckin' afraid of spewin' her guts up."

I nod. That's what she said too.

"But accordin' to Malice, there's a fuckin' lot more that he has to tell us."

"Fuck," Ace hisses. "What the fuck? Why the hell couldn't he tell you? This shit of just waitin' ain't helpin' anyone's anger."

He's right, he should have fucking told me what he had to say. Now we have to wait. That fucker better not take too long. I'm not waiting around much longer.

Fifteen minutes later and the sound of his Harley rumbles as he enters the clubhouse grounds.

"Tell me," I grind out the second he's close.

He nods. "I took Serenity home. I took a cab with her because I didn't want to put her on the back of my bike, not in her state. There was no way I was jeopardizin' her, not the way she was. I'm tellin' you, man, she was fuckin' out of it. She was so withdrawn, it was scary. I've never seen her like that before. It was as though she knew somethin' wasn't right, but the drugs were too fuckin' strong so she just withdrew into herself."

My jaw aches with how fucking hard I'm grinding my teeth.

"I got her home, helped her drink some water, then put her to bed. I made sure that I left her bedroom door ajar so I would hear if she moved in the night. I was fuckin' scared, the way she was. It was fucked up, and I didn't know if she'd get worse."

The raw fear in his voice is real. He truly was worried about her.

"I went into the spare bedroom. Just as I took my boots off, I heard a car pull up outside. I fuckin' knew it was that cunt, Eric. She'd told me that night that she was goin' to end it with him. She knew he wasn't for her. She rarely saw him, and whenever she did, he was way too fuckin' pushy about them bein' together."

"He was goin' to hurt her," May growls.

Malice nods. "He entered the house, but he wasn't alone," he tells us. "He didn't get a chance to do anythin'. The moment the cunt saw me, he high-tailed it out of there, those two fuckers with him. I never saw them before and haven't seen them since. But I'm sure that cunt can tell us who they were."

I can't control my body. My feet are moving before I even register what's happening. I also hear Mayhem filling Malice in on what went down with Serenity and how she was beaten by those fucking assholes.

That red haze is back, but this time, there's no beating it back. I enter the outbuilding and see the fucker chained to the chair.

"What...?" He trembles. "What's going on?"

"Who do you owe money to?" I rumble.

He shakes his head. "I can't. They'll kill me."

My chuckle is mirthless. "What the fuck do you think we're goin' to do?"

He shakes his head. "You don't understand. They'll go after my family."

"You put your hands on my woman. There is no fuckin' mercy for you," I snarl. "You have a choice: you either start talkin', or I'm goin' to force you to talk. Take your fuckin' pick."

He glances around the room, his eyes wide and filled with fear, but it's not enough. He's not going to give up whoever the fuck hurt Serenity. That's fine. It's time for me to start my payback. I move quickly, and the fucker swallows hard.

I've only ever done this once before, and I did it when I was a fucking teen, when I needed to get the guy who was mauling my sister away from her. Thankfully, she was seventeen and he was thirty, so if he'd gone to the cops, he would have been in trouble, especially as he was the fucking school principal.

I curl two fingers and start on his right eye, close to his nose. I press hard, moving the eyeball to the center of the socket. Eric is screaming and thrashing around, but I don't stop. I dig my fingers into the socket. It doesn't take more than ten seconds for me to pop that fucker out. The optic nerves are severed, and the cunt is hysterical.

"Holy shit," Mayhem breathes. "What the fuck, Shadow? Where the hell did you learn that shit?"

"Now, we'll try this again. Who the fuck do you owe money to?"

"The Albanians."

I breathe deeply, needing to take a moment before I go at him again. If I do, I'm going to kill him without getting all the answers I need. The Albanians are into sex trafficking, prostitution, and bookies. I doubt he owes them for drugs, because in New York, they don't have much of a drug business.

That's because between us, the Irish, and the Italian's, we own the majority of the drug trade.

"The night you drugged Serenity," I growl. "Who were the two men you entered her house with?"

He once again shakes his head.

"You have another eye, and I'm more than happy to fuckin' rip it out. If that doesn't work, I'll take every single tooth you have."

"Yes," he cries. "It was the Albanians. That's what I owe them. I promised them Serenity, but when Malice was in the house, we left. They say I owe them two hundred grand as they weren't going to go against him because they know he has deeper ties than they do."

I glance at my brothers and Malice. All of them are watching the cunt with disgust. I want this over and I want it over with now.

"What's their names?" Ace demands. "The two men you were with the night you went to sell her—what are their names?"

Eric begins to tremble. "Amar Prifti and Roel Mehmeti," he stutters. "Please, they're going to kill me."

"Who's the men who hurt her?" Mayhem snaps. "There were three of them."

"Amar, Roel, and Roel's brother, Roan. Please, you have to understand. I didn't have a choice."

"I'm goin' to make a call," Ace tells me, and I

know that he's going to call Makenna Gallagher, the head of the Irish Mafia. If anyone knows where we'll be able to find those cunts, it's her. She knows everyone, and if she doesn't, she'll know someone who does. We'll have those assholes by the end of the week.

"Oh, you had a fuckin' choice alright," I hiss as I edge closer to him. "You shouldn't have fuckin' tried to sell her. Now you're goin' to die, and those cunts who hurt her are too."

"Please," he whimpers. "Please don't do this."

I reach for my knife. I'm going to have fun. I'm going to carve him up like a Thanksgiving turkey.

He screams as my blade slices across his cheek. "No," he cries.

"Scream and cry all you want," I taunt as I swipe my blade over his face once again. "Hell, beg and plead until you're hoarse. I'm not going to stop. Not now, not fuckin' ever. You see, the woman I love was hurt because of you, and I'm never goin' to let that slide. I have no fuckin' mercy for you. You're goin' to die and it's goin' to be painful. So buckle up, bitch, we're just gettin' started."

I chuckle when Mayhem moves to his back and starts to carve that up. There's no way in hell that I'll be able to control myself and not sink my knife in deeper than I should. My rage is coursing through me. I want this shit over with so that Serenity doesn't have to worry about him anymore. Mayhem's getting his kicks in where he can.

I'm not surprised. Over the past five years, things have been relatively quiet, and we've not had to utilize our skills much. So whenever the time does strike, we let loose whenever we can.

Mayhem switches out with Malice. The two men are crazy as fuck when they get going, and neither man will let up with this cunt. He hurt their sister and that's not something either will forgive.

I'm not sure how long has passed, but the fucker hasn't stopped whimpering and whining. He's got shallow slices all over his body, and he's bleeding profusely, but it's not fatal—yet. Malice steps back, a sadistic grin on his face, and I have no doubt that either he or Mayhem—hell, probably both—have carved something into his back.

"No more," Eric cries as he bows his head.

I drop my knife to the bloodied floor and his shoulders slump forward. "Dig," I instruct. "Grab his head. He's in need of something to eat," I say, as my fingers curl around his eyeball.

Digger's deep chuckle only adds to the humor. The man has no problem gripping the cunt's head and pulling it backward, all the while opening his jaw for me. With one eye missing, there's no chance he'll be able to see what I'm doing. I push his eye into his mouth, and Digger slams his jaw shut. I chuckle as his teeth cut through the eyeball, causing it to pop.

"Fuck," Malice snarls. "That's fucked up."

No. That's revenge.

The fucker starts to choke, trying to spit it out, but Digger's not having it. He keeps his mouth firmly closed.

I reach for my knife. It's time to end this. I thrust my knife into his side. It's deep, and the blood flows from his body like a damned river. His breathing becomes choppy. It's hard to tell by how fucked up his face is, if he's red and struggling to breathe or not.

But when I slide the knife into his other side, I know he's in serious trouble. From the way his breathing shallows and his muffled scream, I have a feeling he has a collapsed lung.

"You should never have tried to hurt her," I whisper in his ear. "No one hurts her. Not fucking ever." I thrust the knife into his chest, ramming it to the hilt. It's over within seconds, my blade piercing his heart.

He's dead.

One down, three to go.

SIXTEEN
SERENITY
THREE WEEKS LATER

I'm on edge. Today's the day of the exhibit at the museum. It's been fascinating getting all the artifacts and texts together. I've really enjoyed working on the Rise of Industrial America Era. It's been chaotic to get everything done, but thankfully, I've been able to do it. It has meant a lot of nights with little to no sleep, but it was needed. I was so far behind in the preparations that I couldn't put it off any longer. It was hard, especially when I had an exam to take at college too, but looking around, seeing everyone enthralled by each piece of the exhibit, I know it was worth it.

Over the past few weeks, the men have been on edge, and I hate that it's my fault that they are. Graham told me everything, including that Eric is dead. I'm grateful he didn't go into details about how he killed him. I'd rather not have that in my mind. I love him, and I know that he does things I would never do, but I'll never judge him for them. Especially when he's doing them to protect me. The Albanians are in hiding, from what Ace has said, they know that I have affiliations to the Fury Vipers.. Apparently, Kinsley's best friends with one of the most feared people in the US, and having the entire Irish Mafia after you isn't something anyone would want.

It doesn't make me feel safe. Knowing that the men who hurt me are still out there is a scary feeling. No matter how much Makenna and Ace believe that the Albanians won't touch me, I can't shake the feeling that they will. I mean, two-hundred-thousand dollars is a lot of money to lose. I'm not stupid; I know that people will do stupid shit whenever money is concerned, and I just don't see how they're going to walk away from that sort of money. My gut is screaming at me. Something is coming, and I'm so damn fucking scared. I'm on edge constantly. I have such a soul crushing fear that I can't think straight.

"Are you okay?" Esme asks as she sidles up beside me.

She was pissed when she returned from her parents' and found out that I had been hurt. She wanted to know why I never called her. But when she discovered that it meant that Shadow and I had got together, she was over the moon.

"Yeah, just lost in thought," I reply. "What about you?"

Things between her and Harry are truly over and she's starting to move on. I'm proud of her and will be by her side every single step of the way.

She nods. "Better. It's been hard to walk away from something I dreamed about having, but I know it's the right thing to do. I can't take the constant lies and cheating. He broke something in me. I'm paranoid. Every time I see him on his cell, I'm thinking that he's talking to another woman. I can't trust anything he says anymore. I'm done, and I need time to move on and better myself." She takes a deep breath and smiles. "I still want to be a mom and a wife. I'm just not in any rush to do so. I'd rather go into a relationship knowing my worth than be treated the way Harry treated me."

I saw how paranoid she'd get with him. It really did affect her in ways that changed who she was deeply. I'm happy that she's finally realized she's so much better without him. It's going to take some time for her to work through everything, but no matter what, she's not alone.

"I'm proud of you," I tell her, needing her to know that I'm right here with her.

She leans against me. "Love you, Seri. I'm so sorry I wasn't there when you needed me. I suck."

I laugh. "No, you don't. There wasn't anything you could have done. I had Tavia and Effie, not to mention Graham. You needed the space. You're here now and that's all that matters."

She links her arm through mine. "This exhibit is amazing. You've done a great job. Everyone's talking about it. Not to mention Shadow is reading every single word on each piece."

I noticed. He's taking his time and going through every bit of information. I love that he's taking an interest, but I never expected him to go this in-depth. "He's amazing," I breathe.

She smiles. "You're so in love," she says. "I'm happy for you, Seri. You deserve this. I know how much you've liked him. I'm just happy that he pulled his head out of his ass and realized just how amazing you are."

My cheeks flame at her words. I love that she always has my back and will always want the best for me, and vice versa.

"What's your plan for the rest of the evening?" I ask her, wondering if she's coming back to the club-house with me or if she'll be returning home.

She shakes her head. "I have no plans. Why, what are you thinking?"

I grin. "Want to party? The girls and I are going

back to the clubhouse and partying." I wasn't sure if I should, but Graham assured me that I should have fun and let loose. Especially as I've been working hard. He promised he'd look after me if I drank too much.

"Sounds like fun. Besides, I haven't hung out with the girls in a while. Are you sure it will be okay for me to come with?"

I roll my eyes. "Like I'd party without you."

Her laugh is soft but filled with happiness. I'm not the only one who needs to let loose. She does too. She's been through a lot of heartache the past few weeks and just needs to unwind.

"Peach," I hear the deep, gravelly voice.

"I love that he calls you that," she whispers. "I'm going to mingle. I'll see you in a bit." She presses a kiss against my cheek. "You've done an amazing job, Seri, and I'm so damn proud of you. You've worked your ass off and it shows. Congratulations on an amazing exhibition."

Graham's arms slide around my waist just as Esme walks off. "She's right, it's fuckin' amazing. Proud doesn't even come close to what I feel right now, babe. You're so fuckin' smart and creative. You've shown people a way to enjoy what you love without making them bored. You've managed to get everyone's attention, and your boss needs to give you a damn raise."

I giggle. "I'm not sure if that's on the cards right now," I tell him. "But hopefully in the next year or so." I turn into his arms and smile up at him. "You seem to be enjoying yourself."

His brown eyes are filled with so much love, it takes my breath away. "So fuckin' proud of you, baby."

"You're such a smooth talker," I reply, my voice a little husky. I run my finger along his shirt. I'm still in awe that he dressed up. And not only him, but the other brothers did too. "You look handsome."

"Babe, seeing you in that fuckin' dress, I've been hard as fuck all night. The moment we're home, I'm goin' to fuck you senseless," he growls into my ear, causing heat to pool between my legs.

Before I'm able to reply, we're interrupted by people wanting to congratulate me and talk to me about some of the items that are on display. Graham doesn't complain. No, his hands tighten on my hips, and he gives me a wink and moves away, letting me do what I need to.

It takes me another forty minutes before I'm able to breathe without someone popping up and asking questions. Whenever I move around the room, someone is there asking me questions or wanting to praise me for the job I've done.

I glance around the room, and it's as though a magnet is pulling me when my gaze collides with

Graham's. The heat in his brown eyes has butterflies swarming in my stomach and my heart racing.

God, I want him.

He flashes me that sexy as sin grin of his and my knees weaken. God, I love him so much. He's infiltrated every fiber of me, and I don't want to shake him loose.

I make a beeline for him, unable to hold back. He has this pull over me that I can't deny. Nor do I ever want to.

I reach for Graham's hand and tug. I still have a cast, and it's annoying, but I'm getting used to it.

"Seri, is eveythin' okay?" I hate that there's worry in his tone but also love that he's so protective.

"I need your help," I tell him as I pull him toward the back of the museum. I weave through the throngs of people, not once letting go of his hand until we reach the room which has been converted into my office. It's not the biggest room in the building, but I'm content with what I have. It's homely, although today it's a mess. It has been since I was hurt. I just haven't had time to clean it.

"Babe," Graham growls once I close the door behind us. "You gotta tell me what the fuck's goin' on."

I turn and stare at him, and I see the worry and fear in his eyes. My heart swells.

"I love you," I tell him, letting everything I feel shine in my eyes. "So much."

He moves quickly, pulling me into his arms and kissing the breath from me. His hands slide down to my waist, and he pulls me into his body, his cock thick against my stomach. I wrap my arms around his neck, loving the fire his fingers make as they move along my body.

"Graham," I moan, my body heating at his touch. I've never felt so connected to someone. It's not just sexually with him, but mentally and emotionally. He consumes every single piece of me. I'm so aware of him and can feel and sense whenever he's near. The air always crackles, my heart races, and the blood pumps through my veins faster. It's as though there's a fire inside of me whenever he's around. The love I have for Graham is soul-consuming, and I wouldn't have it any other way.

"Tell me what's wrong," he says, his voice gravelly and low.

"I need you," I whisper, pulling at his clothes. "I ache for you, handsome. I need you."

Those brown eyes of his darken with lust, and his nostrils flare. "Peach," he growls. "You sure you want to do this?"

I don't answer him with words. I reach for his zipper, my gaze solely focused on his. I'm panting as

I free his cock. I fist it, which has him hissing. My panties are soaked, I'm so damn needy.

"Please don't make me beg," I whisper as I begin to pump his cock.

He slants his lips against mine as he thrusts into my hand. His fingers curl into my hair. I don't give a fuck if it looks like we've had sex. I don't give a damn what anyone thinks. I just need him. I'm that damn horny.

His tongue slides past my lips, and his grip on my hair tightens. He swallows my whimper and continues to savage my mouth. This kiss is so intoxicating that I'm lost in it.

I tighten my hand around his cock, our mouths still fused together. I love that he's giving me everything he is. That he's not holding back from me. I pump him harder. My man loves sex. He fucks me into oblivion every single night, but he takes his time when doing so, making sure I come multiple times before he does. That can't happen right now. I need him close before he fucks me, because the way I'm feeling, the pressure that's building inside of me, I'm going to detonate the moment he thrusts his cock inside of me.

He thrusts into my hand, his cock throbbing under my touch. He's thick and hard. As much as I'd love to sink down to the floor and take him into my mouth, we don't have time. But when we get home...

now that's a different story. He can have me any way he wants me.

He pulls back from the kiss, and I instantly feel bereft. God, I need him. His hands slide to my hips and he pulls my dress up, bunching it around my hips. I'm gasping for breath as he leans forward and runs his lips along my jawline and down to my neck. Within seconds, he's got the band of my panties and is tearing at them. The sound of material ripping can be heard along with my heavy breathing. He tears them from my body, shoving the ripped material into the pocket of his pants.

"Gonna fuck you now," he growls, lifting me into the air. I release a strangled squeal as I wrap my legs around his waist. He spins us around and pushes my back against the door, his cock thick against the entrance of my pussy.

"Please," I whimper.

His grin is filled with cockiness and lust as he pulls me down onto his cock. I groan when he bottoms out inside of me. God, he's so fucking big. I love the feel of him stretching me, the way the pleasure has a slight tinge of pain to it.

"Yes," I cry as he pulls out of me and slams into me again. "God, Graham, more."

His hands on my waist tighten, his fingers digging into my skin. "Fuckin' made for me," he grunts as he fucks me.

"All yours," I moan. There's no denying it. I've been his for the past five years. We were just too stupid to see it.

"Mine," he snarls, his thrusts hard and fast. "Gonna love you til the day I die."

My heart races as my breath comes out in pants.

"Always," I tell him, loving how much he loves me and that he's not afraid to show or tell me.

"Too fuckin' right," he says.

"You're mine," I reply huskily. It's only fair that if I'm his, then he's mine.

His eyes darken and that cocky as fuck smile forms on his lips. "Yeah, babe, I'm yours."

He rotates his hips and powers into me. It's as though the last of his control has snapped. With every thrust comes pain, and soon it morphs into pleasure.

"Yes," I hiss as I wrap my casted arm around his neck and press my other hand to his shoulder, giving me leverage to fuck him back. I'm meeting him thrust for thrust with as much passion and need. It's raw and carnal. Every time Graham and I have sex, it gets better and better. We're learning about one another, finding out what makes each other tick, and he knows exactly how to work my body until I'm screaming his name as I come.

I look into those beautiful eyes of his, and all I see is love, adoration, and lust. There's no better feeling than having the man you love look at you with so much emotion. "Love you," I breathe.

He captures my lips once more, kissing the very last breath from me. Our pace is relentless, both of us going hard and fast. There's nothing better than being with him. God, I never want this to end.

He pulls back, and the only noise you can hear in my office is our heavy breathing and the sound of our flesh connecting.

"Gonna need you to come for me, Peach," he grunts, his fingers clenching around the flesh of my hips.

My toes curl around his waist as I feel my pleasure rising.

My body arches back and my head bounces off the door. One of Graham's hands slides from my waist up my body, leaving goosebumps in its wake, until it reaches my neck. His hand tightens around my throat.

"Please," I moan at him, my head starting to feel a little woozy.

"Mine," he growls as he thrusts harder into me. "All fucking mine."

Yes. His. All his and he's all mine.

His fingers flex against my throat, giving me time to pull in a ragged breath, before they tighten ever so slightly.

"Nothin' better than you," he grunts. "You're my fuckin' everythin', Serenity."

"Graham," I cry as my pleasure reaches its boiling point.

He pistons his hips harder, and there's no way I can hold off any longer. He's fucking me so hard my head is banging against the door with every inward thrust.

I detonate. "Graham," I rasp, as my orgasm shatters into a million pieces.

"Fuck, fuck, fuck!" he growls as he explodes inside of me. He buries his head into my shoulder, his breathing ragged. "Fuckin' hell, babe," he snarls. "Almost blacked out, I came that fuckin' hard."

I rest my head against his shoulder and giggle. "I love you," I tell him through my laughter.

His hands tighten around me. "Love you too, babe. Never fuckin' doubt it."

I look up at him and smile. God... How the hell did I get so damn lucky?

SEVENTEEN
SHADOW

"And where the hell did you disappear to?" May asks as he comes to stand beside me.

"Seri needed help with somethin'," I tell him, not once taking my eyes off my woman. She's so fucking beautiful and so damn graceful.

"Bet she did," he retorts through a snort. "Is that what we're callin' it these days?"

I ignore the fucker. I'm not telling him shit. He's a nosey asshole who just wants to know everyone's business. He can get fucked. The little shit tried to warn me away from her. I still haven't forgiven him for that crap yet.

"Is she walkin' with a limp?" he asks through a chuckle.

"Fuck off," I snarl.

"Man, chill, I'm just messin' with you. I don't

think I've ever seen her so fuckin' happy in my life. That's down to you. Thank you. I was wrong. I couldn't think of a better man for her than you."

I swallow past the lump in my throat. Fuck. Now he's forgiven. "'Appreciate that, brother," I say thickly.

"What happened to Serenity's hair?" Storm asks with a smile as he stands in front of me. "It was up when we arrived. Next thing we know, she's walking funny and her hair is down."

These assholes are pushing it.

"That's because she's still sore and she's got a headache. She needed help taking out the pins that held her hair up. Not that it's any of your business, right?" the little woman to our left spits at him. Her eyes are flashing fire and there's a look of sheer disgust on her face.

"Esme," I greet with a smile. She's Serenity's best friend. She's feeling protective of my woman right now, especially as she only found out about what happened to her yesterday.

Storm flashes her his panty-dropping smile. The man has a way with the ladies. He never fails to pull them. "Sorry," he says. "Was just messin'. We love Seri and she's family. How about I get you a drink to apologize?"

Esme's not having it. She crosses her arms over her chest and glares at him. "You talk about all the women in your family that way? Kind of weird that you want to talk about their sex lives." She pauses, a sweet smile on her lips. "No doubt you're struggling in that department." She struts her ass up to him and pats his shoulder. "Don't worry, it happens to a lot of assholes."

My shoulders shake as I press my lips together. Fuck, Esme is not one to mess with. She may be five-foot-two, but she has no problems going toe-to-toe with Storm. I glance at Mayhem, who's struggling to contain his laughter.

"Enjoy your evening, gentlemen," she says as she flips her long red hair over her shoulder and walks away.

I chuckle as I see the lust and confusion in Storm's eyes. He's never been turned down before. I fucking love her for that.

"The hell?" he growls. "Who is she?"

"That," Mayhem says, laughing, "is Serenity's best friend. What the fuck did you do to her, Storm? I've never seen the woman take an instant dislike to someone before."

He slides his hands into his pockets and shrugs. "I've no fuckin' idea." He turns in the direction that Esme just strutted off in, and I see the interest on his face. Hmm. This'll be interesting. "Maybe I should—"

I lay my hand on his shoulder. "Leave her be," I

tell him. "She's comin' to the clubhouse once this is over. You can grovel to her then."

It'll be fun to watch. From what Seri told me, Esme has just come out of a relationship and she's focusing on herself—whatever the fuck that means.

"So you didn't fuck in her office?" Mayhem questions, his brows rising in question.

"What's it to you?" I grunt. "What Seri and I do is none of your fuckin' business."

He raises his hands in surrender. "Christ. What the fuck, man?"

Storm shakes his head. "He's protective of her. He won't have anyone saying shit, and that includes askin' questions. The fucker hates sharin' her time with anyone. I'm surprised he's not stuck by her side tonight, especially with all these people around."

I flip him off. Fucker.

May chuckles. "That explains why he's so fuckin' on edge. He hates that there's other people takin' up her time."

I glance between the two of them. "You done?" I ask, not entertaining their shit.

The two of them laugh. Assholes.

"When is this ending?" May questions. "I love Seri, but fuck, man, this isn't exactly my thing. I've shown my face, I've supported her—that's a lot more than her own fuckin' family have done," he snarls.

Yeah, I noticed that. They claim to be close yet only Octavia is here, supporting her sister.

"That's because I didn't invite them," my woman says as she lays her hand on my back. "I appreciate you coming, Mayhem, I really do. You don't have to stay," she says softly as she presses a kiss against his cheek. "Go home and take Effie with you. She's itching to touch some of the display work, and if she does, I'm kicking her ass." She grins. "Besides, it's ending now. Everyone will be leaving soon."

He chuckles. "Yeah, she's like a damn magpie," he says. "I'll keep an eye on her, but there's no way we're leavin' until this is over. She'll have my balls if I even suggest it."

Seri giggles and turns to Storm. "What did you do to my best friend?" she questions, her tone filled with annoyance.

He lifts his shoulder and shrugs. "No idea. We were talkin', and your girl came over and went off."

Seri narrows her eyes. "Funny. Twice you've seen my girl, and twice you've pissed her off."

Storm's eyes narrow. "Third time's a charm, right?"

She shakes her head. "Third strike and you're out." She crosses her arms over her chest. "I've never seen you piss anyone off, yet with Esme, you've done it twice. Why?"

He runs his hand through his hair. "I've no fuckin' idea. I don't remember meetin' her before."

I wince. That's no doubt why she's pissed.

"Look, Storm, she's my best friend. I don't want her to feel as though she can't come to the clubhouse because she'll run into you." She glances to her right and sighs. "I've got to go." She lifts up onto her tiptoes and presses a kiss against my lips. "I won't be long. We'll go home, get drunk, and then you can have your way with me," she whispers so that only I can hear her.

I watch her leave, unable to take my gaze from her ass as it sways.

"Christ, Storm, what the fuck did you do to the girl?" Mayhem asks.

But I can tell by the look in his eyes that he has no idea. It's going to bug the fucking shit out of him until he can uncover exactly what the hell he did to piss the woman off.

He clenches his jaw as he glances around the room, before stopping on the woman in question. "I'm goin' to find out," he says and makes a beeline for her.

"That's not going to work out well," Mayhem says, his voice filled with glee. "Now, I'd better go find Ef before she gets light fingers."

I chuckle. The woman is crazy on the best of days. Once again, my gaze finds my own woman.

She's smiling as she talks to a group of people. It's as though she can feel that I'm watching her. She lifts her gaze to mine, and without missing a beat, she gives me a blinding smile. My chest warms. Fuck, I'm a lucky bastard. The sooner this is over, the fucking better.

Two hours later and the entire museum is empty. Everyone has long gone and it's just my brothers, their women, Esme, Serenity, and I left. We were going to leave, but when Octavia asked about cleaning up, Seri confessed that she'll be here tomorrow doing it all alone. Well, that wasn't going to happen, and everyone sprang into action. Now, the place is spotless, Seri has fixed the displays, and we're about ready to leave.

"Two minutes," Seri says. "I just have to grab my keys, put the trash away, and then lock up. Why don't you wait outside. I won't be long," she tells us.

Not having to be told twice, we exit the building. My gut is screaming at me, and it has been for the past hour or so. I can't put my finger on why or what, but fuck, something's not right. I can feel it. Minutes tick by and that feeling intensifies.

"I'm goin' to check on her," I say, glancing at Storm.

"I'll come with," he says. The man knows me better than anyone. "What is it?" he asks as we make our way back into the building.

I shrug. "I dunno. I can't put my finger on it. My gut's screamin' at me."

He nods. "You go—"

His words are cut off by a high-pitched scream.

"Fuck," I hiss, my feet moving quickly as I follow the sound.

Storm is on his cell, and he's right beside me, following the sounds of Serenity's cries. "May, go around the back. Something's happenin'. Seri's screamin'."

My blood runs cold when Serenity screams. It's blood curdling, hoarse, and filled with so much fucking pain that it takes my breath away.

"Get off me," she cries, her words loud and clear. She's letting me know where she is. I'm just thankful she's alive and that I listened to my gut and came back inside.

As I quicken my pace, moving through this fucking museum, her screams gets louder. It's a sound I'll never fucking forget.

Her screams rent the air, and it's fucking torture not being able to get to her. Suddenly, there's silence. Utter fucking silence. We run toward the back exit. The door's open, and I hear grunting and the sound of flesh hitting flesh.

"Get the fuck off her," I hear Mayhem snarl.

I run outside, my blood pumping, anger whipping through me. Serenity's lying on the floor, unmoving, blood coating her face. Three fucking cunts are going at it with Mayhem and Digger.

"I got the other one," Storm grunts. "You get your woman."

I don't hesitate. I drop to my knees at her side, my fingers going to her throat, where I feel the strong strum of her heartbeat. I release a harsh, strangled breath. She's alive. Fuck, she's alive. "Peach," I say as I turn, pushing her hair from her face. "Baby, open your eyes."

Slick liquid coats my hand as I push her hair away. The cut that she had on her forehead is back, and this time it's deeper, longer, and jagged. She's covered in blood. I fucking hate that this is the second time I've seen her like this. Fuck. No more. I can't see this shit again. I'm close to losing my fucking mind as it is.

Her eyes flutter open. "Graham," she whispers, her voice hoarse. "You found me."

I frame her face with my hands. "Christ, babe, you nearly gave me a fuckin' heart attack," I whisper back, tears stinging the back of my eyes. "You're goin' to be okay," I promise her. "I swear to you, baby, we're goin' to get you patched up and seen by the doctor. You'll be fine."

"I hurt," she croaks. "Don't leave me."

I press my lips against hers. "Not fuckin' ever," I growl. I'm not leaving her.

I hear sirens and look to Storm. The fuckers who hurt her are on the floor. "Effie called an ambulance," Mayhem tells me.

I swallow hard. Thank fuck for that. "Take my truck," I tell Storm as I reach for my keys and throw them to him. "Put those cunts in the back and take them to the outbuilding. Get out of here. No one touches them until I do."

He nods as he catches them and starts to move. "It'll be done. Take care of your woman. We'll meet you at the hospital," he tells me, and he, Digger, and Mayhem lift the fuckers and move to my truck.

I hear the sound of my truck's engine and it's followed by the rumble of pipes. They're leaving. Good. Now where the fuck is that damn ambulance?

Two hours later, we're in hospital and the doctors and nurses have looked her over. They tried to make me leave but that wasn't happening. Fuck no. I promised her I wouldn't and I'm not going to break it. They don't like me in the room, that's on them. She's my woman and I'm staying right here. Thankfully, they got to work and did whatever the fuck they needed to. Now we're waiting on the results on the blood test. They want to make sure she wasn't drugged due to how groggy she is.

"You good?" Dig asks as he stands beside me. Octavia's at Seri's bedside, her hand in her sister's, but Serenity's unconscious, and the doctors haven't

208

told us why. She fell unconscious while we waited for the ambulance and hasn't woken up since. All the doctors have said is that she'll wake when the time's right.

That's no fucking help and doesn't ease my worry.

"I'm good," I say through clenched teeth. It's a fucking lie. I'm nowhere near good. I want to kill the cunts who hurt her. I also have a feeling they're the three bastards who broke into her house and beat the shit out of her the last time too.

"Once she's awake, we're goin' to make those assholes pay," he growls. "Ace called. He had Malice come to the clubhouse. The three guys are the cunts Eric owed the money to."

My jaw locks. I fucking knew it. I'm relieved they're the same ones. It means that it's just the one enemy, and those bastards are going to die the moment she's awake.

"I'm goin' to take Tavia home to get some sleep, then bring her back in the mornin'. By then, Seri should be awake," Dig tells me. "You'll swap and end those fuckin' cunts."

I smile. "Damn fuckin' straight I will."

He slaps my back and moves to his woman, who instantly puts up a fight, but Digger's not having it. He helps her up from the chair and they say their goodbyes before leaving. Octavia called her parents, but they're not in the country—they're on vacation. That's why they weren't at the museum. Her brothers are currently out of state working, but they're arriving tomorrow.

I take a seat by her bed, her hand in mine and my lips pressed against her knuckles. I fucking hate seeing her lying in a hospital bed. It's the worst fucking thing in the world. I close my eyes and breathe.

I need her to wake. I need to know that she's okay.

"Graham," she says hoarsely a while later.

My gaze moves to hers and I see that she's watching me. "You're awake," I breathe.

"I'm sorry," she tells me. "I didn't see them. They were waiting for me in my office."

Fuck. I should have stayed with her. I should have made sure she was okay. "My fault, babe. I shouldn't have left you alone."

Her hand tightens in mine. "Not your fault. It's not, Graham. But thank you for finding me."

I close my eyes again. The fear of almost losing her takes my breath away. Once we were on the way to the hospital, Mayhem had Cruz and Raptor return to the museum. They found an unlocked van in the parking lot. It had rope and tape in the back. Those fuckers were going to kidnap her and no doubt sell her.

"I'm so fuckin' glad I came back inside," I say thickly. I could have lost her today.

"Love you," she tells me. "So much."

I blink, trying not to let the fucking tears fall, but Christ, I almost lost her. "Love you, baby."

The door opens and the doctor walks in. "Ms. Michaels, how are you feeling?"

"Okay. I'm tired and sore," she tells him.

He nods as he edges closer to the bed. "The results of the blood test came back. There's no sign of drugs."

I breathe a sigh of relief. That's good.

"Your hCG levels are high," he says.

"What's that?" I ask, wondering what's going on. "Is she sick?"

The man smiles at me. "No, sir, she's not sick. Ms. Michaels is pregnant. The levels indicate that she's relatively early in her pregnancy."

I turn to my woman. Her eyes are wide, and her lips parted. Our gazes collide, and I see the fear in her eyes.

Pregnant?

Fuck. I could have lost them both.

Anger whips around me like a cloak.

I tamper it down. Right now, I need to be here for Seri. She looks scared. I hate that she's worried. No matter what, we're going to get through this.

EIGHTEEN

SERENITY

I'm stunned by the doctor's words. Pregnant? How the hell did this happen? "But..." I begin, unsure as to what to say right now. "I'm on the pill," I croak.

My heart won't stop racing. I can't believe this is happening. I'm nowhere near ready for children. I have so much to achieve before I can even think about the future. I know without a doubt that I want to spend my life with Graham. There's no other person who I'd love so deeply as I do him. But kids? God, I feel sick.

"I take it this was unexpected?" the doctor questions, looking between Graham and I.

I can't breathe.

Graham's strong hand tightens around mine.

"Yes," he replies. "Is the baby okay?" he asks. "She was hurt," he says thickly.

I stare at our joined hands, fear coursing through me. I'm so utterly confused. I have an overwhelming sense of dread yet fear that something could have happened to my baby. God, I'm so damn confused. What should I do?

"Ms. Michaels' pregnancy is in the early stages. We'll just have to hope for the best."

I close my eyes as tears sting. I could lose the baby?

The doctor talks about signs I should look out for and what could happen if a miscarriage were to occur. He also tells me that with me being so early, it could be okay. It's just a lot to take in and I'm not sure how to react.

"Peach," Graham says softly once the doctor has gone.

I shake my head. I'm too scared. What if he doesn't want the baby? Then what? Hearing him say he doesn't will break my heart. I don't think it's something we could survive.

Does this mean I do want the baby?

It's so fucking frustrating. I'm too drained to even comprehend what I'm feeling. My emotions are all over the damn place.

"Baby, please look at me," he says.

It's the pleading in his tone that gets me. I open

my eyes and see him hovering over me, his brown eyes filled with love and worry. "No matter what, we're goin' to be okay."

I shake my head. "You don't know that," I whisper, my throat constricting as the tears I've been trying to keep at bay come to the surface. "You don't know that, Graham. I could lose this baby and I didn't even know I was pregnant. How is that possible?"

His eyes close and he releases a harsh breath. "Listen to me, baby." His voice is thick with emotion but holds authority. "You're goin' to be okay. You both are."

Tears spill over as a sob bursts from my chest. "What are we going to do?"

His expression softens. "Ah, baby," he whispers as he climbs into the bed and pulls me into his embrace. "You're scared?"

I nod. "Fucking terrified," I say through my tears.

His arms tighten further. "So am I," he confesses. "I know nothin' about babies. But far as I can see, we've got a fuckin' family full of people who will help if and when we need it."

I press my head against his chest, listening to his heart beating. "I had so many plans, so many dreams."

His lips touch my head. "You're goin' to accomplish every one of them, Seri. No matter what it takes. We'll tick each and every one of them off your list."

"I'm scared, Graham. I don't know what to do. I never meant for this to happen."

He tilts my head up so that I'm looking at him. "I know you didn't. Did you think I'd blame you?"

I shrug. "I'm so overwhelmed, I can barely think straight."

"That's okay, baby, we still have time. Loads of it. The question is: do you want this?" There's no anger or accusation. It's just a question, a normal, everyday question, and I love him for not putting pressure on me. For not telling me what he wants but asking how I feel first.

"I think so," I say softly, hating that it's not a definitive answer. "Do you?"

He presses his lips against mine. "I want everythin' with you, Seri, but the most important thing is that I have you. I don't give a fuck what that comes with. As long as you're by my side, I'm happy."

My tears fall thicker and faster. God, this man. "How did I get so lucky?" I ask.

His chuckle is deep and throaty. "Trust me, Peach, I'm the lucky one."

"Stay with me?" I ask, feeling my body start to drift into Slumberland once again.

"I'm not fuckin' leavin'," he growls.

I smile. I'm so damn lucky to have a man who loves me the way he does.

"Sleep, baby, I'm right here," he promises me.

My eyes close, and it doesn't take long until I'm fast asleep in the arms of the man I love.

My body is warm, and I know it's from the alcohol. An excited buzz is running through my veins. I can't wait to get home. Tonight has been a success, and I'm so damn happy. It's taken a lot to get everything organized, but the exhibit was awesome, and I have a feeling we'll have more people come during opening hours to see it.

I throw the trash into trash bags and leave them in the little kitchenette we have here. Tomorrow morning when the cleaner comes, they won't have much to do, as the girls and the brothers helped me clean it all up. I appreciate that they took the time to do that.

I'm humming along to a song I heard earlier. I only know the tune, not the lyrics, nor do I know what the song actually is. I'm in a world of my own as I finish the last few bits I need to do before I can leave. I gather the paperwork and move toward my office. My cheeks heat as I remember how much fun Graham and I had in here earlier. God, I can't wait to go home and have fun all over again. Nothing feels better than having Graham inside of me.

I enter my office, placing the paperwork on the desk,

and reach for my keys that are on the table so that I can lock up and go home. I hear the floor creak behind me, and my entire body freezes.

It's not Graham.

No, if it was him, my body would feel electrically charged and on fire, as it does whenever I feel him around me. It's not him. But someone definitely is behind me. I hear their deep breathing, can feel their breath on my neck. Their presence isn't a great one. It's as though the air has been sucked out of the room and darkness has settled in its place.

I bring my keys between my fingers, ready to lash out at any moment. It's a trick that all women know. One we use whenever we're walking when it's no longer bright outside. We don't have much to protect ourselves, but keys are a great on the spot weapon if need be. A sharp jab to the face will stop your attacker coming for you for a split second so you can run and get away as fast as possible.

I spin on my heels, and the bravado I had vanishes when I realize it's not just one person—no, it's three—all three men I have seen before. The ones who hurt me in my home. A home I haven't returned to since I was beaten.

"What are you doing here?" I ask breathlessly.

The asshole who's the leader, grins. "I told you I'd be back. Eric's vanished and my money's gone. That means there's only one person left to get me the money. You."

I shake my head as the asshole edges closer to me. "No," I say, my fingers curled tightly around my keys. "I don't owe you a dime," I spit. "You assholes think you can sell me? Think again. I'm not going quietly, and there's no way in hell you're getting out of here alive."

The asshole laughs. "Oh? And why is that?"

"The Fury Vipers won't let you," I say through clenched teeth. I fucking hate the slimy grin he has.

"They're outside, and they have no idea what's going on inside here. By the time they come looking for you, we'll be long gone."

No. That's not going to happen. I'm not giving up without a fight.

"Shadow will never stop looking for you. Eric's gone, and you three are next." There's absolutely no doubt in my mind that the moment Graham finds out I'm gone, he'll search everywhere he can to find me. And he won't stop looking for me or for them.

His eyes flash with uncertainty but he quickly masks it. "Oh, you're fucking a biker, now? Why am I not surprised," he growls as he strikes out, his fist smashing against my cheek. The force of it sends me crashing to the floor, my head bouncing off the edge of my desk on the way down.

I cry out as pain erupts in my temple.

It hits me. Graham's outside, and so is Octavia, Esme, Effie and the brothers. The only way they'll know that I'm in danger is if they can hear me. There's more of *them than there are of these assholes. If I scream loud enough, someone will be able to hear me.*

"Shut your fucking mouth," the bigger of the other two snarls. "You make a sound again, you'll be in a hell of a lot more pain than you already are."

I scream, the sound coming from deep within my lungs.

"Cunt," he growls as he fists my hair and drags me up from the floor. "I warned you," he snarls. His fingers in my hair tighten to the point I'm crying out once again.

"Shut her up," the main guy instructs. "It's time to go before we're heard. If those Vipers find us, we're fucking dead."

The asshole who has my hair fisted starts to move. He drags me along the floor like I'm a fucking animal.

I kick and scream, twist and turn, trying my hardest to get the asshole to release me, but it's no use. He's got a good chunk of my hair in his hands and he's not going to let go.

My vision darkens as he continues, and I know that unless he releases me, I'm going to pass out. The pain in my head is almost too much to bear. But I can't stop fighting. I need Shadow to hear me. I'm praying that he does.

I continue to scream, not caring what those assholes do to me. If they get their way and take me, there's no way I'll ever be returning. They'll sell me.

I feel a cool breeze blowing through the corridor, and

I realize we're close to the back exit. I release one last scream as the asshole pulls me outside. My back scrapes against the dirty ground and a cry spills from my lips.

"Get the fuck off her." I hear the snarl of Mayhem.

I release a sob. They're here. God, they're here.

I'm pushed against the wall, pain erupting from my face once again. God, I'm in so much pain. I lie on the ground, unable to get up.

Within seconds, I hear the best sound in the world. "Peach," he says, pushing the hair from my face and turning me to face him. "Baby, open your eyes."

I look up at him. "Graham," I whisper. "You found me."

He frames my face. "Christ, babe, you nearly gave me a fuckin' heart attack," he replies. "You're goin' to be okay. I swear to you, baby, we're goin' to get you patched up and seen by the doctor. You'll be fine."

"I hurt," I tell him. I can feel my body sinking into the abyss that's calling me. "Don't leave me."

He presses a kiss against my lips. "Not fuckin' ever," he promises me on a growl.

"Baby, wake the fuck up," I hear the growl and feel someone pushing me. "Please, Seri, open your eyes."

I blink at the harsh light. "What happened?" I ask once I see Graham.

"You were dreamin'," he says. "Fuckin' hell, Peach, you scared the crap out of me."

I press closer to him. "I'm sorry," I say softly, hating that I worried him. "Thank you for coming for me." It could have ended a whole lot worse than me being in hospital with a contusion on my head.

His arms tighten around me. "Babe. I swear, you're safe." His hand slides down to my stomach and rests there. My breath catches. "You both are."

With Graham, I've never felt safer. I know that if I ever need him, he'll be here. Not just for me but for our baby.

God, we're having a baby.

I bring my hand and place it over his, right above where our baby is growing. He intwines our fingers and presses a kiss against my head. "Love you, Peach."

I close my eyes, my head resting against his chest. "I love you," I reply.

I feel content. I'm safe and I'm happy. With Graham, I have found my happy place.

NINETEEN
SHADOW

"You good?" I ask Preacher as he gets out of his car.

He's been MIA for the past few weeks. We thought the moment Tyson was released from the hospital, Preach would return home, but he didn't. He called Prez and told him he'd back in a few weeks. That was two weeks ago, and today, he's finally here.

"Never better," he assures me, and I stare at him, wanting to see that for myself. But yes, he's right. That darkness he had when Pepper was pregnant is gone and he seems lighter.

I slap his back. "Good to have you home, brother."

He grins. "It's fuckin' good to be back. I appreciate you comin' to speak to me, man. I'm sorry I wasn't there when those cunts came for Seri."

I grin. "That's okay. They're currently tied up and waitin'. You're not the only one who just got back. Seri was released from the hospital this morning. I haven't had time to fuckin' go at them yet."

"That's somethin' I'd love to see. You think Seri would be okay with Tyson?"

"Absolutely," I reply instantly.

My woman may be pregnant and scared about our baby, but that doesn't mean she doesn't love all children. She'd be honored that Preach trusts her with his son.

"Come on, everyone's waitin' on you. I wanted to check in with you before the party, see where your head was at and if you needed anythin'."

"'Preciate it, brother. Honest to fuck, down to my fuckin' bones, I couldn't ask for a better godfather for Tyson."

I stare at him in shock. What the fuck? "Wanna repeat that?" I rumble.

He chuckles. "Shit went down with me, and you were there. Your woman was there. You have no fuckin' idea how much that meant. Not to mention, neither you nor Seri left me alone while I was gone. If it wasn't you callin' to check up, it was Seri. Although, her updates were a fuck of a lot better than yours."

I chuckle, knowing exactly what updates Seri has been sending him. Pictures of Ace and Eda's twins going after Cruz. The man is soft as fuck and the kids are all drawn to him, but Ace's twins are heathens, and they don't leave him be. One night while asleep, the twins decided to use Cruz as a canvas and started to paint him. I've no fucking idea where they got the brushes or the paint, but when Cruz woke up, he was covered in different colors. It was hilarious, especially as they painted his beard green and red.

"Cruz still hasn't managed to get that paint out of his beard."

"That wasn't paint," he tells me, chuckling. "Seri and Effie have been givin' those twins the ammunition to fuck with people. It wasn't paint they used. It was fucking hair dye."

I press my lips together. I fucking knew Seri was involved in that shit. She was acting too damn innocent not to be. "How the fuck do you know?"

He smirks. "They've had it planned for a while. I overheard Effie on the phone one day. She was writin' out a shoppin' list of what they needed, and Seri purchased it."

"Yeah, well payback's a bitch," Effie says from behind me. "Cruz doesn't help matters. That fucker thinks it's funny that the twins constantly go for our boobs. So no. Payback's a bitch, and your woman is a genius at coming up with ways to get back at people."

I'm not sure if that's a threat or not, but I don't care. "Where is Seri?" I ask.

Effie grins. "Clever man. Just don't get on the wrong side of her and you'll be fine."

I have no intentions of doing so.

"She's inside. The kids are making sure that she's okay and Sera is asking questions about her exhibit."

I smirk. "She's goin' to take her there, isn't she?"

Effie shakes her head. "No. May growled and grunted that Seri isn't going back there today. So Digger's taking her."

Preacher chuckles. "Just what he'll want. No doubt he was bitchin' about bein' there last night."

"Trust me, man, that exhibit was the shit. The only asshole who bitched about it was Mayhem. Which is why I think he should take the kids," I say, looking directly at Effie.

She beams at me. "You, Shadow, are a genius. Let me go speak with Seri. I'm sure we can get the kids to work Benji."

I chuckle as she practically skips into the club-house. I turn to Preach. "You ready, brother?"

He nods. "Fuck yeah. Let's get Tyson introduced to everyone."

The moment we walk into the clubhouse, everyone cheers. I notice Effie and Seri with their heads together, no doubt conspiring to get Mayhem to bring the kids to the museum.

"Ruby," Seri calls sweetly to her eldest niece.

The girl in question turns from the crowd of people looking at Tyson and moves toward her aunt. The three girls get their heads together and talk. It doesn't take a minute before Ruby's grinning and moving toward her sister, Serafina.

"You up to no good again?" I ask my woman as I reach their table.

She gives me her best innocent look. The big eyes, parted lips. She's fucking adorable. "Who? Me?"

I chuckle. "Babe, I know all about your antics. Cruz's beard ain't ever goin' to be normal, is it?"

She bites her lip and shrugs. "I got the wrong dye," she whispers. "I got the permanent one, not the semi-permanent."

I chuckle. "He fuckin' loves it, babe. The shit he's gettin', he's eatin' it up. The man craves attention and you both have given him a reason to have some."

Seri smiles. "Phew. Okay, that's not too bad. I was feeling kind of guilty."

I drop down onto the seat beside her and wrap my arm around her shoulders. "You doin' okay, babe?"

She nods as she rests her head against my shoulder. "I'm good, handsome. I'm really happy that Preach's home. This is where he belongs. I hate that he went away, but I also understand that he needed to."

"Seri, do you need any pain pills?" Octavia asks as she comes to stand by the table.

Serenity gasps as she turns to her sister. "Oh, shit, Tavia. What the fuck?"

Tavia's eyes narrow. "What?" she asks. "What happened?"

"Your hair. Why is it so gray? There're at least five strands," she whispers, sounding horrified. "What happened?"

Octavia's eyes widen. She turns on her heel and rushes out of the room.

Effie chuckles. "She's going to be pissed."

Seri shrugs. "That'll teach her for being so damn nosey and trying to look through my chart this morning."

I've never seen Serenity move so quickly. Even with her broken arm, she managed to grab her chart before Octavia could open the first page. The sisters stood off against each other but ultimately, Serenity won. We agreed that we wouldn't tell anyone about the baby until we were both one hundred percent okay with it, and even then, not until Seri was past the twelve-week mark.

With Seri pregnant, it puts three of the old ladies due to give birth this year. Eda, Effie, and Seri. There are more kids than most of us can keep count of, but fuck, my brothers are happy and that's all that matters. The kids are fucking hilarious, especially the twins—who turn one next month. Those little heathens are going to be pranksters when they're older, especially if they continue to allow Serenity and Effie to corrupt them.

"Serenity Lynn Michaels," Octavia hisses when she returns, her eyes swirling with anger. "I do not have gray hair."

Seri smiles sweetly at her. "In this light you do," she responds.

"Ugh," Tavia growls. "You're a pain in my—"

"Ass," Serafina finishes for her mom as she comes to sit with us.

"Sera," Octavia, Seri, and Effie reprimand together.

"Oh, honey," Seri says softly. "We don't say that, okay?"

Sera's eyes widen. "Daddy does."

Well, ain't that the truth. "Your dad's an adult," Octavia sighs. "When you're an adult, you can say that too, but, baby, we try and say nice words, okay."

Sera nods, presses a kiss to her mom's cheek, and runs away, no doubt hoping she won't be reprimanded again.

"She's a kid," Seri says. "She doesn't understand why she can't say those words, especially when the other kids can."

Octavia sighs. "Do you think I should let her?" she asks, biting her lip.

Seri shakes her head. "Hey, you're an amazing mom. You do what's best for you and Digger. No one else gets to dictate how you parent. You hate it when anyone says a swear word. Some may argue ass isn't one, but you don't like it. So no, I don't think you should. Because it's disrespectful to you."

"Don't think I could have said it better myself," Effie says. "She's right. You do whatever you feel is right. I won't let Elouise say whore, even though that's what everyone calls the women. It's just something I find disrespectful, especially now that I know the women personally."

Seri nods. "I totally agree with that one," she sighs. "But the men say it and it's not going to change, so all we can do is explain to the girls that it's not nice to call someone it." She pauses for a beat, turning her head to the side. "Unless absolutely necessary," she says, a smile on her lips.

Effie chuckles. "That's true, but back to you, Tavia. You're her parent. You know what's best for her, and we'll all respect whatever decision you make. You don't want her to say ass, then if she does, we'll remind her that she's not allowed to say it."

Ah, now it makes sense as to why all three women reprimanded her when the little girl said the word.

"Please don't doubt yourself," Seri says. "You're an amazing mom. Just believe that."

"She's right," I say. "You know what a good mom is because Mama Michaels set the example. You have no idea how not to be one. Trust me, you're fuckin' amazing. Sera and Ruby are lucky to have you as theirs."

Tears fill her eyes, and she looks away. "Thank you," she whispers. "It's hard sometimes."

Serenity and Effie share a look. "Octavia, sweetie," Serenity says. "Are you okay?"

Tavia wipes away her tears. "Sorry, I'm just emotional."

"What's wrong?" the women ask.

She sighs. "Ruby and I butted heads today. She wants to go to a party, but Tate said no, so when I told her, I got the blame. She told me she hated me."

I wince. Octavia has a soft heart, which is why her and Digger are perfect for one another. No doubt having Ruby tell her she hated her, hurt. Dig needs to tell his daughter he was the one who made that decision. Fuck. I couldn't imagine having your kid say that, especially when you love them.

My cell rings. I press a kiss against Serenity's head and get to my feet. It's an unknown number.

"Yeah?" I answer as I step outside of the clubhouse.

I'm greeted by silence.

"Hello?" I say when I hear someone breathing.

"Graham," a brittle voice says.

My muscles tense when I realize who the fuck is calling me. "What the fuck do you want?" I snarl.

"My appeal was rejected," she says.

"Good," I spit. "You deserve to fuckin' die inside that jail, Jessa. The sooner you do, the fuckin' happier I'll be."

"I deserve to be here?" she says, her voice shrill. "You should be here. You failed her, Graham. Had you protected my baby girl, she wouldn't be dead right now. You've always failed everyone. You're a useless motherfucker, Graham Davis. You always have been and always will be." Her voice is getting louder with each word she says. "You're the reason she's dead. Not me. You."

Christ... It's been years since I've spoken to this bitch, and yet when I get my life sorted, she calls me, trying to pull me into her fucking bullshit.

"You're done," I grunt, pissed that we're even having this conversation. It never changes. She'll never admit that she's a cunt.

"Graham," she begins.

I've had enough. "Goodbye, Jessa. I hope you rot in fuckin' Hell. Lose my number. You call again, I'm hangin' up." I end the call and take a deep breath.

Cunt. The fucking bitch has gone too far.

TWENTY

SHADOW

Having that fucking bitch call me has left a red haze over me. Christ, I had gotten over that shit. Finally started to move on from the darkness of my past. But fuck, Jessa... The bitch can't leave me be.

I walk back into the clubhouse, my anger from the call bubbling up inside of me. I need to unleash the demons that haunt me. There's only one way to do that. The cunts are currently waiting for me in the outbuilding.

"Handsome, everything okay?" Seri asks me as she sidles up beside me.

"Fine," I say through clenched teeth as I try to keep moving.

She steps in front of me. "Sounds like it. How about we try it again?"

I spear her with a glare. I can't do this right now. Fuck. "Not now."

"Graham," she says softly, reaching out to touch me.

I brush her hand away. I can't deal with this now. "Fuck's sake, Seri. I don't need you up my fuckin' ass," I say a little too fucking loudly, and the entire clubhouse descends into silence.

"What?" she hisses. "Are you for real right now?"

I run a hand through my hair. "Fuckin' hell, woman. What the hell is your fuckin' problem? I told you there's nothin' wrong, but you just won't fuckin' stop."

"You're angry," she whispers. The entire clubhouse is watching us. Fucking great. "Graham, I just want to help."

"You want to help?" I hiss. "Then fuckin' leave me be, yeah? Just fuckin' stop. Christ. Some fuckin' breathin' room would be good."

She sucks in a sharp breath, her eyes wide and her lips trembling. I can't fucking stop the shit spewing from my mouth. I watch as she swallows hard. "Okay," she whispers. "If that's what you want. I just hate that you're so angry."

"Leave it, yeah?" I snarl, not wanting to speak about this shit. "It's got nothin' to do with you."

Wrong fucking thing to say. Hurt slashes through her features, but just as quick as it came, it's gone. She stands tall and looks at me without a fucking ounce of emotion. "Sure," she replies, her voice deceptively calm and fucking cold. "We'll leave it."

She turns on her heels and moves through the clubhouse toward the stairs. I want to go after her. I should fucking follow her. But I can't. My feet are rooted to the spot. Christ. Have I just fucked up everything?

"What the fuck, brother?" Storm says as he grabs my shoulders. "What happened?"

"Jessa," I bite out.

"Fuck," he snarls. "The fuck did that bitch want?" he questions as we walk back out of the club-house and toward the outbuilding. "You've fucked up. You realize that, don't you?"

I glare at the fucker. Of fucking course I know that I've fucked up. I've never, not fucking once, spoken to her like that before, and I shouldn't have done so now. She's right to be hurt and pissed. I'm a fucking bastard for how I spoke to her. But right now, I'm too angry to do anything about it.

"You know what Tavia went through, brother," he says quietly. "You think either of those girls are goin' to put up with someone talkin' to them the way you did?"

"You're a fuckin' asshole, Shadow," Mayhem snarls from behind me. "You know what, I was wrong. You're nowhere near fuckin' good enough for her. That woman was gutted. You fuckin' bastard. You gutted her in front of everyone. Make you feel better, did it?"

"May," Ace says. "Let's get these fuckers dealt with and then you can sort this shit out. He'll apologize when he realizes he fucked up."

May chuckles. "She's not goin' to be here when he realizes that. Seri isn't goin' to take the shit you dealt her. I wouldn't be surprised if she vanishes. Hell, I'll fuckin' help her if she needs it."

I ignore his words. I can't focus on them right now. I'll lose my damn mind if she leaves.

Storm's hand tightens on my shoulder. "Get these fuckers finished, get your woman safe, then go and grovel," he tells me. "You need to sort your shit, though, brother. That was fuckin' bad."

I grit my teeth. Fuck, I know it was. I have so fucking much to apologize for. She doesn't need the added stress of me being a dick. She's pregnant and injured. I'm a bastard.

I walk into the outbuilding and see the three men tied to chairs. All three heads rise as we enter. The stench of piss is fucking putrid. Someone needs to drink more fucking water.

"I see you've made yourselves at home," I say as I get nearer, not in the least bit surprised when I find it's the biggest fucker who pissed himself. It's always the big fuckers who are the most scared.

"What do you want?" the eldest of the three men growl, struggling against his bindings.

"You hurt my woman—"

"Not yours anymore," Mayhem says under his breath.

"Not once but twice," I continue, ignoring the fucking asshole. "You knew she had ties to us, and you still felt the need to try and take her. Why?"

"She owes us," he says, his accent thick. "Two-hundred-thousand dollars we were going to get for her. The deal had been made. Artyom Solovyov took a liking to her that night in the club. He wanted her for himself."

Acid burns in my gut. Everyone knows who Artyom Solovyov is and what the fucker does.

"You sold her to him?" Mayhem snarls. "You fuckin' sold her to that monster?"

The man shrugs. "I do not care for the woman. You all do. That's a shame. You all know that once a deal is made, it has to be honored."

I snort. "Honored? You've no fuckin' idea what honor means."

His eyes flash with anger. "You disrespect me?" he says, pulling against his bindings. "Do you know who I am?"

"We do," Ace drawls. "And we don't give a fuck.

You don't sell women, and you certainly don't sell our fuckin' women."

"You're goin' to pay for hurtin' her." I grin, reaching for my knife.

"She should have just done as she was told," the cunt growls. "Had she, none of us would have been in this position."

No, she'd have been thousands of miles away with fuck knows who.

"Wrong answer," I snap as I step forward. "She should never have been touched." I slice my knife along his ear, cutting into it. The asshole doesn't even flinch. He sits still and waits. He's been trained. It's a shame that his training is for nothing.

Mayhem and Digger move, each one taking a man. It's time to fucking end this shit. Once these cunts are dead, then Serenity is safe, and we won't have to worry about anyone coming for her. These fuckers want their money, which means Artyom Solovyov isn't in business with them anymore.

I slice through his skin, much like I did with Eric. The sight of blood is like a balm to the anger that's coursing through me. Every single swipe of my blade is deep and deliberate. This fucker is going to bleed out.

I glance over at Mayhem and smirk when I see he's carving the man up like a fucking pumpkin. Mayhem loves to hurt people. It's who he is. He's been that way since he witnessed his woman bleeding out from the bullets she took thanks to our old prez. He took out an entire organization because he believed it was them who hurt Effiemia. He'd do anything to protect those he loves, and Seri is one of those people.

Digger's already finished his asshole. He didn't waste any time, just slit the fucker's throat. Now he's bleeding out, struggling to breathe. Effective and downright painful.

I look down at the cunt and see he's slowly fading. He's lost a fuck of a lot of blood. I flick the knife in my hand and thrust the blade into his eye. The howls that come from him are horrific and animalistic.

"Christ, Shadow," Ace hisses. "The fuck—you have an obsession with eyes?"

I chuckle. "Only for those wantin' to hurt my woman." I pull my blade out and do exactly the same to his other eye. "He put his hands on her. For that, he's paying with his life." The pain he's feeling is because of the fear he instilled into her. The nightmare she had last night is something I'm not going to forget. The whimpers and cries that I heard as she slept were more than enough to scar me.

Pulling the knife from his eye, I slice it along his throat, much like Digger did to the other fucker. Once he's bleeding out, I step back and smile. It's done. They'll never be able to hurt her again, and if that cunt Artyom Solovyov comes for her, I'll take him out too.

"Go see your woman," Ace tells me. "You're gonna have a fuck of a lot of grovellin' to do, brother. We've got this."

I don't need to be told twice. I move out of the outbuilding and toward the clubhouse. Every fucking step that I take is filled with dread. I have a feeling that Mayhem was right and she's gone. Now that the red haze has slipped away, I realize just how badly I fucked up.

She didn't deserve me taking my anger out on her. She deserves to be treated with love and respect, and the way I spoke to her was neither. Ace is right, I have a lot of groveling to do.

I quickly shower in the outhouse, needing to get clean so I don't scare Serenity.

The moment I enter the clubhouse, everyone turns to me. The women all glare at me and turn their heads. Seems it's not just Seri I'm going to have to get on good terms with. Those women are lethal when they get going, and there's nothing worse than having them hate you. If they're against you, you're fucked. But my main objective is to get my woman on side and apologize. Fuck, I need to do more than apologize. I screwed up.

I walk up the stairs and move toward my room.

"She's not there," Preach tells me, his words filled with anger. "Dunno what the fuck happened, brother, nor do I care right now, but you fucked up speakin' to her that way. She's said she's givin' you the space you need, and she'll be back." He's got Tyson against his chest as he glares at me.

"You let her leave?" I hiss.

He raises a brow. "Pretty sure you did that yourself. What was it you said again? Oh yeah, it was, 'Fuckin' leave me be, yeah? Just fuckin' stop. Christ. Some fuckin' breathin' room would be good.' Not to mention, you said she was up your ass." He shakes his head. "Tell me, brother, has she asked about your past?"

I grit my teeth. "Once."

"Did she push you to talk about it?" he asks, knowing fucking full well she wouldn't. I shake my head. "No, didn't think so. The woman has been at your side—fuck, at my side—even though she's hurtin'. She's been nothin' but fuckin' solid. And you treated her worse than you'd treat a fuckin' whore. She was right to leave."

I scrub a hand down my face. "What do I do?"

He looks at me with disgust. "Figure out what you want, 'cause, brother, that shit happens again, she'll never forgive you." With that bit of information given, he goes into his room, closing the door behind him.

I enter my own room and sit on the bed. Fuck, I'm such a fucking bastard.

Preacher is right. I need to sort my shit out. Which means working through my past. I already know what I want, and it's Seri. Jessa fucking Davis isn't going to ruin it.

TWENTY-ONE
SERENITY

My heart hurts. I know that something's happened, but having Graham push me away hurts my heart. I hate that he's going through something and I can't help him.

"Are you okay?" Tavia asks as I reach for my suitcase.

I sigh, trying my best not to cry. I'm not going to break. Not now, not in front of anyone. "Yeah, I'm just tired. I'm going to go home, have a bath, and then sleep for a bit."

She presses her lips together. "Do you think that's a good idea?"

I throw clothes into the bag, moving around the room to ensure I have the essentials I need. "Yeah, it's the best thing to do. We're practically on top of each other, have been for almost two months now.

We need the space. I'm not leaving forever. I just want to take tonight and be alone."

Saying the words hurts. Sure, I'd be okay with being away from him if it weren't on these terms. The things he said to me were in anger, but I can't help but wonder if he actually meant them.

"But, Seri—" she whispers.

I shake my head. "Trust me," I ask her. "I'm safe. The men are gone, and I'm safe. I'll call you the moment I get home, and knowing you, Tavia, you'll be messaging me throughout the evening to ensure that I'm okay."

She rushes forward and pulls me into her arms. "I hate this," she says, fighting her tears. "I hate that he spoke to you that way. You didn't deserve that."

"No, I didn't. There was no fucking need for it and I'm angry that he did it in front of everyone, but I also know that he's dealing with something and he's pushing me away because of it. I'm not leaving because I'm done. I'm going to give us space so that we can regroup, calm down, and then when we do talk, it won't be filled with angry words."

Well, that's what I'm hoping for. I don't want to fight. God, I'm beyond exhausted, and having to deal with this shit on top of everything else is just too much. I'm still reeling from the attack last night and discovering that I'm pregnant. I don't have the energy to wrap my mind around anything else.

"Be safe," she tells me when I've finished packing.

"Aunty Seri." I hear the deep voice of Cage. "Are you okay?" he asks me.

I smile. I love my nephew. He's his father's son for sure. So sweet, kind, and intelligent, but don't fuck with him. "I'm okay, honey. I'm going to go home for tonight and get some sleep."

I watch as his jaw clenches. "Let me give you a ride," he says, his tone brooking no argument.

"That would be great, honey. I wasn't sure how driving with a cast would work," I say through a laugh, though I was determined to do it. I need to get away from here for a bit.

He shakes his head. "You're gonna call me honey forever, ain't ya?"

I smile as I walk over to him. I press a kiss against his cheek, having to reach up onto my tiptoes to do so. "Perks of being your aunt, Cage. I'm allowed to do that."

He takes the suitcase from me and wraps his arm around my shoulders. "Fine, but that's just 'cause you're the shit. I wouldn't take it from anyone else."

My smile is wide, and I lean into him. I'm so damn lucky to have such amazing people in my life. My nephews—Rush included—are some of the greatest men I know.

"Seri, you good?" Rush asks as we step outside, Cage moving toward my car.

"Yeah, sweetie, I'm good. I'm just going to go home."

Like Cage, his jaw tightens. "He's my brother," he says quietly so that no one else can hear him. "But he lost a lot of my respect for talkin' to you the way he did."

I turn so that I'm facing him. "Listen to me, sweetie. I love you," I whisper, knowing that he doesn't hear it much. He rears back, his brows knitted together. "But I need you to understand that sometimes, people have bad days—"

"He shouldn't have spoken to you like that," he snarls, cutting me off.

I nod. "He absolutely shouldn't have. We both know that sometimes we do things we don't mean. I try not to judge people on the things they do, but how they fix them. Tomorrow, we'll see how Graham reacts. Then I'll judge him. But he's your brother. He'll have your back no matter what, and sweetie, you'll have his."

He glares at me, his arms crossed over his chest. "I'll have his back," he says, "in everythin' 'cept how he treats you."

My heart feels like it's going to burst.

"You, my sweets, are amazing. I'm so fucking proud of the man you have become."

He swallows hard, his gaze sliding away from me. I get it. The shit that happened years ago has affected him, and he's still not feeling as though he belongs. Bullshit. He fucking belongs.

"Rush, sweetie, you're so damn unsure of yourself that you can't see just how much we all love you. You did what you had to do, and while you hurt a lot of people, you saved Ruby. No one is mad at you anymore. Octavia is fine, and that woman loves you something fierce, as do I."

His eyes brim with water, and I hate that I've made him cry.

"Please look at me," I ask softly. He slides his gaze back to me. "I love you, Rush. You're my nephew, just as Cage is. Just as Ruby and Serafina are my nieces. You are my family."

He pulls me into his arms and holds me tight. I press my head against his chest, wrapping my arms around his waist and holding tight.

"Thank you," he says gruffly. "You're the first person to tell me that."

I swallow hard, bile rising in my throat. If I ever find his parents, I'm going to kill them. How can anyone do that to a child? How can you not let your child know that you love them? I shake my head, trying to rid the pain of how I feel and look at my nephew. Just like Cage, he's taller than me. Then again, most people are.

"Do you have to stay here?" I ask, and he shakes his head. "Cage is bringing me home, and I wondering if you wanted to come too?"

He grins as he slides his arm around my shoulder. "Sure—just to make sure that you're okay and the house is secure."

I roll my eyes. These men are so damn protective and sweet.

I climb into the back of the car and Rush slides into the front passenger's seat. Even though these two started off hating one another, they have a deep friendship, just as Storm and Graham have. It runs deep. Cage and Rush may not have had the best foundation to begin their friendship, but it's turned into an amazing one.

"Boys," I say once Cage is driving toward my house, "I know you're both upset, and I get it. I am too. But you can't show anyone that. It's disrespectful, and you're both so new to being patched members that I wouldn't want you to cause tension. So please, don't do or say anything?"

I've listened as Effie and Octavia have told me about the way the club works and what they're allowed to do and what they can't. The last thing I want is for my nephews to get into it with Graham and there to be no way back for them.

"Fine," Rush says through clenched teeth. "We won't say anythin'."

I wait for Cage to do the same. I notice that his grip on the steering wheel is tight, and his knuckles are white.

"Cage, honey?"

"Fine," he grunts. "But only for you."

I smile. "I appreciate that, honey."

I hear them both sigh. "You're good men, and I know your dad would be proud of you."

Rush tenses, and I curse myself for saying that. He doesn't see Octavia and Digger as his parents. I feel even more love for the fact he calls me aunty. "I'm proud of you both," I tell them.

"That's 'cause you're the shit," Cage says, laughing. "You'd be proud of us no matter what."

I humph. He's not wrong. As long as they're happy, I'm happy. "Am I not allowed to express my pride for the men you have both become?"

Rush wasn't the only one who had obstacles to overcome—Cage did too. Cage lost his biological mom at the age of thirteen and then discovered who his father was. It was a rough time, but Cage, being who is he, was amazing and took everything in his stride.

The two of them talk as Cage drives us to my house. They sometimes bring me into the conversation, but I'm more than content to listen to them. It's so good to see them smiling and being happy. That's all I want for my family.

Pulling into my drive, Rush puts his hand out for my keys, and I roll my eyes.

"Stay here," he instructs. "We'll check to make sure it's secure and then we'll come back and get you."

I hand him my keys, and he chuckles at my scowl.

Ten minutes later and they're back, Cage getting my suitcase from the trunk while Rush helps me out of the car. Jeez, utterly perfect gentlemen.

"The ladies you two end up with are going to be damn lucky."

"Can you imagine if we start datin'?" Cage says. "Mom will lose her shit."

I laugh. They're not wrong about that. "You're still her baby," I say as I reach for his cheek and pinch it lightly. "She doesn't want to lose you."

He rolls his eyes. "How the fuck is she gonna lose me? I mean, Dad's part of the club and so am I. I'm not goin' anywhere."

"She'll be happy to hear that," I say, not wanting them to go, but knowing that it's selfish to want to keep them here with me.

I walk into my house, and my blood runs cold as I remember the last time I was here. God, I hadn't thought of how I'd react to being back.

"You good here, Aunty Seri?" Rush questions, his gaze scrutinizing.

I nod as I plaster on a smile. "Yeah. I'm going to have a bath, eat something, and then read before I go to bed. I'm still a little drained from last night." Not to mention the baby that's growing inside of me.

He watches me for a beat. He doesn't miss a thing. "You need anything, call me, Seri. I mean it."

I salute him. God, he's worse than my damn brothers. "I promise. If I need anything, I'll call you, Rush. Now go." I shoo him toward the door, Cage laughing as I do. "Go, enjoy yourselves. You need to have some fun."

They both give me a grin, and I shake my head. I've heard the stories, but I don't want to believe them. They like to share sometimes, and the club women are more than willing to have them both.

"Out," I hiss as their grins turn into smirks. "Or I'll start talking about me and Graham."

Their cockiness vanishes and horror fills their eyes. "Don't," Cage growls. "Seri, I swear to fuck, don't you dare. I'm traumatized enough hearin' Mom and Dad go at it; I don't need to add you to the mix."

I smile sweetly at them. "Same goes for the both of you. I don't need to know about your sex life either. So, go, before I start spilling my guts."

They both kiss my cheek before exiting my house, and I can't help but laugh at their eagerness to leave. I hear the engine of the car rumble before they back out of my drive. The moment the car's gone, coldness starts to seep into my bones as the memories of what happened here hit me.

I swallow them down. I can't and won't let those assholes ruin my life. I take a deep breath and decide that I'll eat first and then have a bath.

Maybe tomorrow will be a better day.

TWENTY-TWO
SHADOW

I sit outside her house. I've been here for ten minutes, and I'm contemplating whether or not I should go in. She left because she needed the space, and I want her to be okay, but I can't just sit here. I need to know that she's safe.

As I was leaving the clubhouse, I bumped into Rush and Cage. Fuck, if I thought Mayhem and Digger were protective of her, they have nothing on those boys. I asked them where she was and they ignored me, both of them glaring as they walked past me. Asses. I get it though. I fucked up and hurt their aunt.

I climb off my bike and move toward her house. I'm pissed when I push down on the door handle and the door opens. The fuck? She's home alone; this door should be locked. I glance around and note that we need to get her an alarm system. I need her safe when I'm not around. As much as I love the club-house, there are going to be times when we'll be staying here, and I need to know that when I leave, she's going to be okay.

Silence greets me as I walk through the house. The kitchen is empty, but there's a plate and a mug on the side by the sink. She's eaten. That's good. I continue through the house, but every room I enter is empty. My heart's in my throat, fear coursing through me as I push open the bathroom door. I release a harsh breath when I find her lying in the bath, eyes closed and looking peaceful.

"I know you're there," she says, not opening her eyes. "You're like a fucking bull in a china shop walking through the house."

I chuckle as I close the door behind me and move toward the bath. "Peach—"

She shakes her head. "Don't want to hear it right now, Graham."

I sink to the floor. I want to reach for her, to touch her, but I won't. Her body is tense as a fucking bow. "I'm so fuckin' sorry, baby," I say. "Honest to fuck, if I could take it back, I would. I should have never spoken to you that way. You deserve respect, and the way I spoke to you and the words I said were anythin' but that. I'm sorry."

She opens her eyes and turns to me. "Why did

you?" she whispers, hurt shining in those beautiful eyes of hers.

"Growin' up, I didn't have the family you did—"

"Handsome," she whispers. "You don't have to do this. I know your past is something you don't want to talk about."

Fuck. Even after I've been a fucking bastard, she's still sweet and fucking perfect. "I'm gonna talk about it. You deserve to know."

She nods. "Could I get out of the bath first?" she asks, wiggling her toes. "The water's cold," she says sheepishly.

I get to my feet and reach for the towel.

"Thank you," she says, wrapping it around her body. "Wait for me in the living room. I won't be long."

Fifteen minutes later, she enters the room, a burgundy silk robe on her body, her feet bare as she pads toward me. She looks fucking beautiful, the bruising finally gone from the first attack. Thankfully, there's only a small bruise on her temple, where her wound is.

"Okay, handsome," she says as she takes a seat beside me.

"I lived in a trailer," I tell her as she brings the cushion to her stomach and holds it, almost as if she knows it's going to be a horrific story. Her eyes are open and watching me intently. "My mom was a drunk who had an array of mental health issues. Back then, people like us didn't get the help needed so it went unmedicated. Hell, even if she had the drugs, I doubt she would have taken them."

Her eyes are soft, her teeth pressed down against her bottom lip.

"My dad was a drug addict. Anythin' he could get his hands on, he would. It was fuckin' awful. The two of them would either be at war, arguin' and fightin' all the time, or so fuckin' high they'd be screwin' the brains out of one another. There's no doubt they loved each other. There were more highs than lows."

She smiles at that. "Even if it was drug-induced, it's cool that they were in love to do it. My parents do the same," she whispers.

I nod. "That's true, but the fights were fuckin' shit, Seri. I mean, you could hear them screamin' at each other a block away. It was fucked up." I swallow back the bile as I remember the shit they did to one another. "Mom was the violent one. She'd throw shit; use whatever she could get her hands on."

She licks her lips. "Was it only your dad she hurt?"

I shake my head, and tears fall from her eyes.

"It was a long time ago, Peach," I tell her. There's nothing worse than seeing her cry. "My sister and I would end up at Storm's trailer. His mom was the shit. She reminds me a lot of your mom. She didn't care that we were there. She'd do whatever she could to feed us. But it wasn't much, as she was a single mom with two boys. You've seen Storm, baby, and he's always been big."

She laughs. "His poor mama," she says, shaking her head.

"The years went on, and as we got older, shit got worse. She'd try to take shit out on me and my sister. She put us in hospital a few times," I tell her. I remember the questions we were asked, but back then, things were different. If you came from the trailer park you were labeled as scum and no one gave a shit.

"Cerys was four years older than I was. She hated living in the trailer, and she had big dreams. She was goin' to get a job and move out, find a place and take me with her."

"She sounds amazing," Seri whispers, her tears falling thick and fast.

"She was, and she got her dream, baby. She got away and took me with her. We lasted three months before Mom called her back home. I told her not to go, that we didn't need to go back there, but Cerys..." I shake my head. I've replayed that day over and over in my head, wondering if there was anything I could have done differently, but no matter what, it would have ended up the exact same way. "She went. She wouldn't listen to me. And she took me with her."

"Hey," she whispers as she scoots forward, her hand reaching for mine. "It's okay. You don't have to do this."

I hold her hand tight. "I owe you everythin', Seri, and that's what I'm givin' you. I'm almost done, baby."

"Okay," she whispers.

"When we got to the trailer, Dad was gone, and it was a fuckin' mess. I hadn't seen the place so fuckin' dirty in my life. My mom was off her face. I don't know if she took drugs that day or what, but she was so out of it that her eyes were unfocused. I doubt she could even see straight."

She grips my hand tighter, not saying a word.

"I went to my room, not wantin' to listen to the shit that was about to go down. I put on my head-phones and listened to music, drownin' out the arguin' that was happenin'." I shake my head. "I shouldn't have done it," I growl. "I heard a scream. It was so loud that I heard it over my music." I swallow hard. "I waited, trying to see if it would sound again, but all I could hear was grunting. I got up off the bed and walked out of my room. What I saw was some-thin' I'll never forget. My mom beatin' Cerys to death with the iron."

She gasps, her tears spilling faster than before. "No," she whimpers. "Oh, Graham," she sobs.

"I pulled her off Cerys, but it was too late. The damage was done. I've never seen such a fuckin' mess in my life. Blood was splattered everywhere. It was like I was on the set of a fuckin' horror film." Not to mention, brain matter was everywhere too. My mom beat her with that iron more times than was needed. The doctors said the first blow was enough to incapacitate Cerys. It was the second blow that was fatal. Everything else was just overkill. The bitch hit her seventeen times. There was nothing I could have done. She was killed before I could have gotten to them.

"Please tell me that bitch is in prison," she hisses, those gorgeous eyes of hers flashing with anger.

I nod. "She is. When the cops came, she tried to say I was the one who killed Cerys. There was no way it was me. Luckily, the blood splatter over Mom —" Not to mention the brain matter "—was enough for the cops to know the cunt was lyin' to them."

"What happened? Where did you go?" she asks, blinking furiously through her tears.

"Storm's mom took me in. I was thirteen, and she didn't think twice about takin' me in, even though she was struggling as it was tryin' to make ends meet."

"What happened this morning?" she asks, her voice soft. There's no more anger.

"My mom called," I tell her, and watch that anger flare again. "She was denied parole and blamed me."

"Fucking bitch," she hisses as she swings her leg over my thighs and straddles me. She takes my face in her hands and looks at me. "You do know that she's full of shit, right?"

I palm her ass, my cock thickening. "Yes, Peach, I know. I fucked up though. That time of my life was shit, and I was angry. She blamed me a lot, tellin' me that I shouldn't have brought Cerys to the trailer, that I should have kept her away."

"The woman's blaming anyone but herself. No more," she sighs. "I won't ever let you do it again. The way you spoke to me, Graham, it won't happen again. It does and I'm done."

I pull her into me, her pussy resting on my pants, my cock thick and my hand on her ass. She's not wearing panties. Fuck, I need her. I swallow hard.

"I know," I say, knowing that until we talk this through, we can't get past it. "I knew the moment I said it to you that it was beyond fucked up. I'm human, Seri, and I'm goin' to make mistakes, but I sure as fuck learn from the ones I do make. I swear, it won't happen again."

She smiles. "Thank you for apologizing," she

whispers, pressing her lips against mine. Her hands reach between us and she goes for my zipper. "And for telling me about your past. I know it wasn't easy, and I'm honored you trusted me with it."

I hiss out a breath as she frees my cock and starts to jack me off.

"You're mine," I snarl, thrusting into her hand. "No one I trust more." I take her mouth, needing to taste her. It's been too fucking long since I did. My tongue snakes into her mouth, and I take everything from her. God, I fucking love this woman.

"God," she breathes as she pulls back from me. "I love you, Graham, so fucking much. I need you to fuck me. I'm so damn horny."

I grin as I get to my feet. Her hand releases my cock, and she wraps her arms around my neck. I grip her ass and pull her down onto my cock. She gasps as I thrust into her, bottoming out inside of her.

"I don't want to hurt you," I say as I walk toward her bedroom. With every movement I make, my cock gets deeper inside of her.

Her fingers twist into my hair and she tugs it. "You won't," she moans as my lips touch her neck. "Please, Graham, I need you to fuck me."

I press my lips against hers, needing to taste her. I deepen the kiss when she moans. Nothing will ever be as good as being balls deep inside of her.

I reach the bedroom and lie her on the edge of

the bed, then I start to move. I groan deep as I fuck her hard and fast, our lips still fused together. Christ, I can't get enough of her. I never will.

"Fuck," she cries when I hit deep inside of her. "More," she pleads with me.

Rotating my hips, I fuck her hard, fast, and brutally. Every bit of control has gone. There's no finesse, no sweetness, as I hammer into her like a man possessed.

"Graham!" she cries out as she detonates around my cock. Her pussy walls tighten around me as she comes.

I continue to thrust hard and deep, my fingers digging into the flesh of her ass. The pace is unrelenting, and I'm unable to stop. I'm so close. I need to fuck her, need to claim her. She's mine.

I continue pounding into her hard and fast, my grip tighter than before. There's no doubt my marks are going to be left on her ass. She releases a moan, and I capture her lips once more, needing more. I can't fucking get enough.

"Graham," she breathes as she pulls back, her eyes filled with lust and love.

"You're gonna come for me again, baby," I hiss as I bottom out inside of her.

"Yes," she screams, her body tensing. Her back bows, and she detonates.

Her pussy clenches around my cock again, and I

can't hold back any longer. I thrust once—twice—thrice, and come long and hard, groaning into her neck as I do.

Fuck, I'm completely fucking spent. The woman is my match in every fucking way possible. "Love you," I breathe.

I feel her smile. "I love you too, handsome."

TWENTY-THREE

SHADOW

I bite back a growl as Serenity's hand slides along my inner thigh. We're in my truck because she's too far along in her pregnancy to take on my bike. I grip her hand, stopping it's trajectory toward my cock. Her body tenses, and I know that she's pouting. She's fucking pregnant, and as much as I want to fuck her—my cock is thick and hard constantly around her—I need to do it safely, not lose my damn mind while I'm driving.

She's six months pregnant, and today we have her scan. Seeing my kid is fucking surreal, and I'm over-fucking-joyed that we're having it. Serenity and I spent a lot of time discussing what we were going to do, and in the end, we both agreed that we wanted the baby. I know it's going to take a while for us to adjust, but we'll get there—

together. Today, we're announcing the pregnancy, and I know that she's excited. She can't fucking wait.

I spot a dark parking lot and pull in. I can feel Seri's excitement when I pull her out of the vehicle and skim my hand along her dress.

"This is goin' to be quick, Peach," I tell her. "I'm goin' to fuck you, and then we're goin' to tell everyone the gender of our baby."

She steps toward me. "So this is the pre-celebration," she purrs as she presses against me.

I slide my hands around her waist and kiss her. "This is goin' to be quick," I tell her again as she steps back and pulls her panties down and her dress up around her hips. I can't help but grin as I unbutton my jeans and free my cock.

I bend her over the hood of my truck, her ass in the air, and slide into her tight, hot pussy. I growl low. Whenever I touch her, it fucking ramp up the neediness. She's so fucking tight. I thrust into her, needing to get as deep as I can. Seri moans, the sound reverberating off the parking lot walls.

"More," she pleads.

My hand snakes into her hair and I tug. Hard. Her back bows and she cries out in pain, but it's entwined with a moan. I continue to thrust, each one hard, fast, and precise. This isn't love making, this is about satisfying our needs.

"Please," she mewls, her pussy clenching around my cock.

My release snakes around my spine. I'm close, but I need her to come first.

"Come," I growl, knowing that I can't hold it off if she doesn't. I twist my hips and hammer into her.

She's shaking with need. "Yes," she breathes. "Oh, Graham," she cries.

"Fuckin' come," I snarl as my balls tighten.

Her body bows, her pussy contracts, and she floods my cock. "Graham," she cries.

I thrust into her one last time, burying myself to the hilt, and detonate. "Fuck," I growl. My legs are shaking from the aftermath of the orgasm.

I hold her close to me, making sure I don't put my weight on her. We stay like this for a few minutes, needing the time to recover.

"Let's go home," I tell her as I fix her clothes, along with my own.

I help her back into the truck, a satisfied smile on her face. This is the fucking life.

I SMIRK as Seri comes to sit with me. Instead of letting her take the seat beside me, I pull her onto my lap, my hand resting on her neat bump. "Here she comes," Seri breathes.

Serafina skips into the room, a bright smile on her face. "Daddy, look, I got a new t-shirt," she tells him, playing with the hem of it.

Digger glances down at it and then smiles. "That's nice, baby."

I chuckle. He hasn't even noticed.

Preacher, who's sitting beside him, looks down at the little girl, his eyes widening a fraction before sliding toward us. He raises his glass. "Fuckin' knew it," he says loudly for everyone to hear.

The man was shot two weeks ago. You'd think he'd be taking things easy, but not Preach. He's living life to the fullest while being a single dad. The man's a great fucking father. Tyson's lucky to have him. I couldn't imagine him not being a father.

"Knew what?" Tavia asks.

"Mommy, look," Sera says loudly, pulling at her tee.

Octavia reads Serafina's t-shirt that says, 'My Cousin Lauren is Coming Soon'. Her eyes widen, and she turns to Serenity and I, looking at where my hand is resting. "Really? It's a girl?" she breathes.

Seri nods. "Really."

Within seconds, Octavia has pulled her sister from my arms and the two of them are hugging while my brothers come over and congratulate me.

"Yo, Preach," I hear Mayhem call out, his voice filled with anger.

Preacher looks up from beside me. "What?"

"You got a minute? Need to talk to you, brother," May says, his eyes focused solely on Preacher.

"Brother, whatever you've got to say, you can say now. We're celebratin'."

May shakes his head. "Trust me, Preach, this needs to be said in private."

"How about you say whatever it is now, May?" Ace says.

The prez has spoken, and May grinds his teeth. "Fuck, I wanted to do this in private," he snarls. "When you were shot, Effie realized that your blood type is O Positive."

Preach shrugs. "Yeah, what of it?"

Seri looks at me, and I pull her into my lap once again. What the fuck is going on?

"You know that Tyson's blood type is AB, right?"

Seri turns and faces me, her eyes filled with tears. "Graham," she whispers.

"Baby, what's wrong?" I ask as I frame her face. I also note that Octavia is in Digger's arms.

"Someone with O Positive blood can't be the father of an AB blood type," she whispers quietly so only I can hear her.

"What?" I snarl. "You sure?"

She nods, pressing her face against my chest and sobbing.

"Someone want to tell me what the fuck is goin' on?" Preacher snarls.

"A parent with the blood type O Positive," May begins "can't be the parent of a child with the blood type of AB."

The only sound that can be heard is Seri and Octavia crying. Everyone else is stunned to silence.

"What the fuck you sayin' May?" Preach growls, his eyes wide and his jaw slack.

"I'm sorry, brother, but there's no possible way that Tyson is yours biologically."

Fuck. Fucking Pepper. The bitch is dead and she's still fucking ruining people's lives.

Preacher walks out of the room and toward the stairs. We leave him be. That shit is something he needs to deal with before we can talk with him. Anyone who goes near him now, they're gonna brawl.

"So, who's the father?" Seri asks.

I tense, knowing that I fucked the bitch around that time. I can't be sure when it was, but I do know that I was drunk and fucking stupid, lost in my mind after seeing Seri dancing with some asshole at the bar.

"You?" she asks softly. There's no anger, just softness.

"I fucked her, yeah, but I swear to fuck, Peach, I dunno about that boy bein' mine."

She presses a kiss against my lips. "I think the best thing to do is have everyone take a DNA test and then go from there."

I pull her into me and kiss her. Fuck, I love this woman. No matter what shit I've done in the past, this woman stands by me.

"Come on, Peach," I say as I get to my feet. "Let's go watch a movie."

There's no doubt that once Preach has come to terms with the news, everyone's going to want to know who the father is, and that's shit's going to get complicated.

As shit as it is, I don't want it to be me. Fuck. I'm a bastard, but I don't care.

The second we're inside our room, she's on me. My woman is fucking horny constantly since becoming pregnant.

I palm the back of her head and take her mouth, my tongue sweeping past her lips. A little moan escapes her as I deepen the kiss, my cock, thick and heavy, pressed against her stomach. I grip her hips tighter, pressing against her, careful not to press against the bump that's between us.

"Fuckin' love you, Peach," I say as I reach for the hem of her dress.

Her eyes blaze with love and happiness. "I love you, handsome."

I'm a lucky bastard.

WHAT'S NEXT?

Are you ready for Wrath and Hayley's story?

https://geni.us/FuryVipersWrath

She's unable to move forward... He wants everything with her...

Hayley's determined to have the best life for her and her daughter. Her rules. Her terms.

With her walls firmly intact, she's determined to never feel loss agains like she's felt her whole life.

Sleeping with a patched member of the Fury Vipers was never on the cards.

But one night was never enough.

Their connection undeniable.

Five years Wrath has bided his time, knowing that Hayley was the woman for him.

How can he make her see he isn't going anywhere?

When Hayley and her daughter's lives look to be in jeopardy, Wrath will do everything to ensure they stay safe.

Will Wrath and Hayley get their happy ever after, or will they end before they've even truly begun?

Ruthless Betrayal, Niccolò's and Inessa's story is coming...

https://geni.us/RuthlessBetrayal

**All I've ever wanted is to be loved. He's determined to
make me suffer.**

Growing up within the depths of the Bratva organization,
I've only felt violence and brutality.

Surviving this life I've been dealt is my only goal.

Marrying the underboss of the Italian Mafia was
supposed to be my lifeline.

But Niccolò Caruso is only out for one thing—revenge.

Being a husband was never on his agenda.

When the Bratva comes calling, everything around me
shatters.

My lifeline cut short.

Sometimes love isn't enough.

**Can this dangerous Mafia man find a way to let go of
his grief and protect me?**

Want to catch up with the series, why not read Book 1,

Ruthless Arrangement now - https://geni.us/
RuthlessArrangement

*Haven't read the Made Series yet? Why not start at the
beginning? Check out the series here -* https://www.
brookesummersbooks.com/made-series

BOOKS BY BROOKE:

The Kingpin Series:

Forbidden Lust

Dangerous Secrets

Forever Love

The Made Series:

Bloody Union

Unexpected Union

Fragile Union

Shattered Union

Hateful Union

Vengeful Union

Explosive Union

Cherished Union

Obsessive Union

Gallo Famiglia:

Ruthless Arrangement

The Fury Vipers MC Series:

Stag

Mayhem

Digger

Ace

Pyro

Shadow

Standalones:

Saving Reli

Taken By Nikolai

A Love So Wrong

Other pen names

Stella Bella

(A forbidden Steamy Pen name)

Taboo Temptations:

Wicked With the Professor

Snowed in with Daddy

Wooed by Daddy

Loving Daddy's Best Friend

Brother's Glory

Daddy's Curvy Girl

Daddy's Intern

His Curvy Brat

Taboo Teachings:

Royally Taught

Extra Curricular with Mr. Abbot

Private Seduction:

Seduced by Daddy's Best Friend

Stepbrother Seduction

His Curvy Seduction

ABOUT BROOKE SUMMERS:

USA Today Bestselling Author Brooke Summers is a Mafia Romance author and is best known for her Made Series.

Brooke Summers was born and raised in South London. She lives with her daughter and hubby.

Brooke has been an avid read for many years. She's a huge fan of Colleen Hoover and Kristen Ashley.

Brooke has been dreaming of writing for such a long time. When she was little, she would make up stories just for fun. Seems as though she was destined to become an author.

WANT TO KNOW MORE ABOUT BROOKE SUMMERS?

Check out her website:
www.brookesummersbooks.com

Subscribe to her newsletter: www.
brookesummersbooks.com/newsletter

Printed in Great Britain
by Amazon